A

MOUNTAIN CHRISTMAS

Romance

Wyoming Mountain Tales

BOOK 4

MISTY M. BELLER

This book is a work of fiction and any resemblance to persons, living or dead, or places, events or locales is purely coincidental. The characters are the product of the author's imagination and used fictitiously.

ISBN-10: 1978011962
ISBN-13: 978-1978011960

Dedication

Blessed be the Lord, who daily loadeth us with benefits, even the God of our salvation.

(Psalms 68:19)

Thou wilt shew me the path of life: in thy presence is fulness of joy;

at thy right hand there are pleasures for evermore.

Psalm 16:11 (KJV)

Chapter One

November 7, 1867
Mountain Bluff, Wyoming Territory

The thrill of speed pulsed through Matthias Björk as he leaned low over the horse's neck, the wind whipping the coarse, white mane across his face. He reined the gelding around a boulder, then wove through the scattered pine and spruce trees. He knew from experience the creek would appear ahead once he rounded that cluster of cedars.

The horse dodged right to skirt the evergreens, his muscles bunching as he anticipated the coming leap over water. The animal loved adventure as much as Matthias, unafraid to grasp a thrill wherever he found it.

The trees cleared, revealing the narrow chasm through which the creek ran. He tightened his legs around the horse, lifting out of the saddle to signal Karl into a jump.

But a flash of white underneath them caught his focus. A person?

The gelding had already begun his leap, and Matthias's shift in focus threw the animal off balance. As they soared over the gap between the banks, a squeal sounded beneath them, high pitched like that of a woman. Then a large splash. Had Karl's hooves struck her?

He didn't have time to wonder long, for his distraction had altered the momentum of the horse's jump. Karl's front hooves landed on the far shore, but as his rear hooves should have struck solid ground, the animal's back end seemed to scramble, then sink down as he fought for purchase on the bank.

Matthias leaned forward, trying to use his weight as an anchor to help the horse stay up on the bank. But Karl continued slipping, shifting backward as his hooves clattered against the rock surface of the four-foot cliff.

A scream sounded from behind, then the fury of splashing water. The horse was losing the battle to stay on the bank. Matthias kicked his boots free of the stirrups, scanning the area for the best place to leap off. The chasm containing the stream wasn't more than four or five feet wide, so he would likely be dashed against the rocks on the far side if Karl fell backward.

He swung his leg over and pushed away to the left, trying to land on his feet in the water. His boots hit the icy stream with a splash, but the rocks littering the bottom threw him off balance, toppling him into the creek.

Cold.

Nay, freezing. The frigid liquid stole away his breath and nearly his senses.

But Karl's frantic thrashing helped restore the latter. Matthias scrambled away from the panicked horse, who had landed on his side and was struggling to rise in the small enclosure between the rock walls.

A figure moved on the other side of the horse. A woman standing in the creek bed, hand extended to the flailing animal. "Easy, boy. Don't struggle. Easy, there."

Her crooning seemed to work because Karl stilled. His heavy breathing filled the air as he lay in the water, sides heaving.

The woman approached, still murmuring. As she grabbed the reins, Matthias eased to his feet. Creek water dripped from his clothes and ran down his left side, which had been submerged. Numbness spread through his hands and feet, both from the wintery air and the water, mostly run-off from snow higher in the mountains.

He ignored the bite of cold and eased toward the horse as the woman attempted to maneuver him into a position that would make it easier to stand.

"When he tries to rise, pull him that way." Matthias motioned toward the left bank.

The woman looked up at him as though she'd just now noticed his presence, her eyes piercing with a crystal blue stare. His heart panged. With her blond hair and delicate features, she looked much like his sister probably would now that she'd grown. And Alanna would be about this woman's age, or maybe a little older.

He studied her, but she turned away to urge the horse again. Still, Matthias couldn't shake the power of the woman's presence. Could she be his long lost sister? The only living family he had left? He'd been searching so long, finding her on this remote trail would be just like God's sense of humor.

Yet, a tiny part of him—the part of him that was all virile male—hoped that the beautiful creature helping to extricate his horse from the icy water was not a blood relation. In fact, her elfin features made her almost seem like a woodland nymph, like in the myths of old, the stories his parents had passed down from their Viking forefathers. Of course, the woodland nymphs were only legends, not flesh and blood like this damsel.

"Stand clear!"

Matthias leaped backward at the woman's call, jolting to the present as Karl gave a mighty lurch and scrambled to his feet, assisted by the woman's pull on his reins as she guided him to the only available space in the creek bed.

"Good, boy." She stepped forward to stroke the horse's neck as he heaved, water dripping from his winter coat where he'd lain in the stream.

Matthias moved to take the reins, trying to ignore his own wet clothing and the water sloshing in his boots. "I'll take him."

She handed over the leathers but remained at Karl's neck, stroking the thick, wet hair and crooning.

Her nearness raised all the hairs along his arms, which were already goosefleshed from the chill. He stepped back, away from Karl's head. Away from the woman.

He had to refocus on what needed done. "From whence do you hail?"

She glanced at him, a curious light touching her crystal eyes. "Mountain Bluff. And you?"

"Nowhere." 'Twas his standard answer to that question. Nowhere. Many places. He'd wandered for so many years, he wasn't even sure what it would feel like to belong in a place.

She raised her fair brows, which were almost exactly the color of varying strains of fresh honey. But at the moment, the perfect arch of those brows clearly communicated her wary frustration.

"Nowhere, sir?" If he'd not caught the message portrayed by her expression, the exasperation dripping from her tone said it well enough.

He shrugged. "I hail from these mountains. What are you doing so far from town?" This spot must be at least an hour's trek on foot.

"Gathering herbs."

Now it was his turn to raise his brows. "In winter?"

She studied him as though taking his measure. "My apologies for startling your horse." She turned back to Karl and offered him a final pat, then stepped back.

5

As she moved away, a noise sounded like the squeak of wet leather. Matthias glanced down at the hem of her practical brown skirt as she stepped from the water. "Your shoes are soaked. Do you have a horse to ride back? You can't stay out in this cold long."

"I'll be fine." She hoisted herself up over the bank's edge. Matthias lunged forward to help, but then stopped himself as he was faced with a skirt and shoes that gave no safe place to position his hand to help. She accomplished the feat with impressive grace though, and pushed to her feet.

Matthias gathered both his wits and Karl's reins. "Are you here alone, then? Your husband allowed you to wander so far unescorted?"

"I have no husband. I work for a family there, and as I said, I'm gathering herbs to replenish our supplies."

As she spoke, she scooped up a basket he hadn't noticed on the ground, then rummaged through it, not sparing him a single glance.

But her words pricked Matthias's memory. The last time he'd stopped at Mountain Bluff, Vatti Shumeister had mentioned the woman they'd hired to help Mutti Shumeister with her baking. The lady had been away visiting relatives at the time, but...could this fair-haired nymph be her? He'd pictured a plain-faced spinster, too vinegarish to find a husband, even in this land crawling with eager bachelors.

He eyed her. "Do you work for the Shumeisters?"

She jerked her head up. "You know them?"

He nodded. Vatti and Mutti Shumeister were the closest to family he'd had for years. Other than his sister, of course. Which was why he had to find her.

He turned back to Karl. "I'll need to lead him downstream to a place where the bank is not as steep. Then we'll take you home." If she belonged to the Shumeisters, she had now become his responsibility. And he certainly wasn't going to leave her alone and on foot so far from town.

He left her there and led the horse downstream. They found a place about thirty yards from the woman, and Karl seemed as eager as he was to escape the icy water. But as they trudged back on dry ground, the water squished in his soggy boots. It would be a long ride to Mountain Bluff.

The woman was kneeling over her basket when he and Karl reached her side.

He vaulted into the saddle, then extended his hand. "Give me your basket first, then I'll help you climb up."

She spared him a glance, and the disdain in her eyes made it clear she didn't plan to accept his offer. "I'll return on my own when I'm ready."

He didn't lower his hand. "I can't leave you out here. Haven't you gathered all the herbs you need?" What could she possibly find in this season, with all the plants barren of leaves?

She straightened to her feet and started walking away.

Exasperation simmered in his gut. What was wrong with this woman?

He nudged Karl forward to follow, then reined in when they came abreast of her. "Miss. I'm not leaving you out here. If there's more to gather, tell me and I'll help. Or I can even come back for it." That would be the more pleasant option, given the fact that his toes had already benumbed and his boots had stiffened as though developing a shell of ice.

"I don't mean to cause you trouble, sir." She didn't give him a moment's notice with the words.

He let out a huff. "You're causing me more trouble by refusing than if you'd just hand me the basket and climb on the horse. Not to mention you may have the power to save my damp feet from frostbite if you make haste."

She turned a startled gaze on him, studying his face first, then lowering to his boots. Her shoulders slumped as though she'd eased out a sigh, and she handed the basket up to him.

When his hand touched her cold one, a warmth spread up his arm, washing through him to his toes. He did his best to ignore it as he secured the basket onto his saddle so that nothing would fall out.

She seemed to be experienced with horses as she fit her boot into the stirrup and swung up behind him.

He gave her a moment to settle, then nudged Karl forward. 'Twas harder than he'd expected to ignore the warmth of her behind him, even though she sat with a gap of several inches between them.

She didn't speak, and he allowed an easy silence to settle, enough for him to mull over a few things that had struck him as odd. "It seems like you've ridden a horse before."

He waited. She didn't speak, so he waited longer.

Finally, she said, "Yes."

That was all? He hadn't asked a direct question, but her response was more than short.

"Did you learn to ride after you came to Mountain Bluff?"

"No." At least this time, her answer was more forthcoming, although edging even closer to rude.

But her curt response gave him the impetus to push farther. "Where did you live before coming to this place?"

"My cousin and I came from Pennsylvania." Her voice softened this time, coming out almost meek. And something about the tone sent of pang to his chest.

"Is that where you learned to ride? In Pennsylvania?"

"Yes."

Again with the one-word answers. But she still had that melancholy tone that made him want to cease his inquisition.

Once more the silence settled, and he tried to find his easy rhythm, the peace that always came on the trail, riding through the scrawny pines with rocky peaks rising all around him.

But the calm in his spirit seemed elusive this time. Maybe 'twas his body so stirred from the nearness of such a lovely woman. Or maybe 'twas the fact he couldn't seem to draw her into conversation. Not that he was terribly

9

experienced with women. In fact, he rarely interacted with the fairer gender except for the occasional boardinghouse matron or cafeteria serving girl, and he didn't usually give half a moment's consideration to what they thought of him. But something about this woman made him crave her good opinion.

Or maybe he just wanted to hear that smile in her voice, the one that lit her features when she'd stroked his horse.

"Have you ever owned a horse, Miss…?" He searched his mind for her surname. Had Mutti or Vatti ever mentioned it? She didn't fill in the gap, so it seemed he'd have to ask outright. "What *is* your name?"

"Miss Opal Boyd."

He took in a breath for patience, then let it out. "Have you ever owned a horse, Miss Boyd?" It seemed she would make him force every syllable she would deign to offer.

"Yes, Mr. Björk."

He looked over his shoulder to study her. "How do you know my name?"

She shrugged. "I assumed that's who you were. You didn't introduce yourself, but the Shumeisters speak of you often."

He couldn't help the warmth that flowed through his chest. Not only did they think of him when he wasn't there, but they even mentioned him. But he only allowed a small nod as he turned back to the trail.

10

After another quarter hour, the silence had officially stretched his nerves taught. The land leveled out, opening to a wide valley and open trail. This particular area spread for almost a mile. The perfect landscape to pull Miss Opal Boyd from her reserve.

Perhaps. It might be worth the effort.

"You should probably hold on tighter for this stretch of land."

Her body stiffened behind him. "Why?"

"It would just be a good idea." Let her shake loose a bit if she didn't want to take his advice. They'd start slowly enough that he could make sure she didn't actually slide off Karl's back. But just in case… "Actually, you might do best to hold around my waist."

The noise in his ear sounded like a snort, not something that would escape the mouth of a woodland nymph.

He bit back a smile as he pressed a heel into Karl's side.

The gelding pushed into a canter, and Miss Boyd's snort was replaced with a squeal. He reached to grab her coat so she didn't slide off. At almost the same moment, she gripped the sides of his own coat, jerking him back with the momentum of the horse's speed. He reached for the horn and was barely able to keep them both on the horse's back.

Karl never slowed through it all, and when they'd both regained their balance, Matthias crouched low and gave the horse his head. Miss Boyd had finally taken his advice and now clutched tightly around his waist.

11

The wind whipped at them, bringing an icy chill that made his senses spring to life. The horse's white mane flapped in his face, raising the scent of the wild that always centered him. His mouth found its usual grin, possibly heightened by the pretty woman clinging to him.

Too soon, the end of the valley loomed ahead, and he straightened, easing back on Karl's reins. Behind him, Miss Boyd leaned away, although she didn't release her clutch around his middle.

When Karl settled back to a walk, Matthias turned to glimpse her. Would she be angry? She'd been hard to read, so maybe she was one of those uptight schoolmarms who didn't know how to enjoy a carefree moment.

He turned to see. She was tucked so tightly against him, it was hard to catch more than a glimpse of her grin. She noticed him looking and eased back, not quite meeting his eye. The way her lower lip was tucked in her teeth didn't hide her smile, though. Not when a twinkle lit her crystal blue eyes.

And that twinkle did funny things in his chest. Stirring up a sensation he'd do best to shun.

Chapter Two

O pal slipped from the back of the horse the moment Mr. Björk reined in behind the Shumeisters' boardinghouse. The elegant white gelding had been mannerly, which was more than could be said for its owner. Her legs still shook, whether from the fear of riding pell-mell through the wilderness, barely hanging on behind the saddle, or from the effort of clinging to the horse and man. What kind of rogue was he?

The Shumeisters had always spoken of him in the most endearing terms, almost as if he were their own child. Although this ruddy, broad-shouldered man more closely resembled a warrior than a child, with the golden scruff of his beard and his hair curling at the nape of his neck.

She'd learned long ago that men weren't trustworthy, and his actions on the ride back proved that point well. She certainly couldn't rely on him to protect her sensibilities.

13

He dismounted after her, then reached to unfasten her basket. He handed it over with a roguish tip of his mouth. "Tell Mutti and Vatti I'll be in shortly."

Mutti and Vatti? Did he mean Mr. and Mrs. Shumeister? The strange words rolled off his tongue in the same way the older couple spoke their German. Maybe he was related to them.

She nodded and escaped into the house.

Mrs. S. stood at the work counter when Opal entered the kitchen and looked to be rolling some kind of meat into a pastry. The tangy scents of dill and vinegar wafted through the room, easing the knot in her chest. This place had the power to settle her spirit like no other.

Certainly not like Riverdale, the manor house where she'd lived from birth until midway through her eighteenth year. This was a real home, a place her heart could rest. Find peace. Who would have thought her haven would be this little boardinghouse and bakery in a tiny mountain town tucked in the Western wilderness?

'Twas as Mrs. S. had said, often, God's ways only made sense in hindsight.

The older woman turned to her as Opal placed her basket on the table. "You found ze winter savory plant and ze willow tree? You have no trouble with ze bark?"

"No trouble with the bark." She lifted the cloth covering her basket to reveal strips of bark she'd cut from the willow tree near the creek.

Mrs. S. nodded as she turned back to her work. "Gut."

14

Opal stepped into the large pantry and pulled down the jars where they stored willow bark and winter savory, then added her newest harvest to the scant supply in each. After resealing the lids and replacing the canisters, she tied on her apron and reached for the bowl of dough she'd mixed that morning. It had risen nicely in the constant warmth of the kitchen.

An image of the fair-haired warrior flashed through her mind. "Oh, I met Mr. Björk while I was out."

Mrs. S. stopped her work and looked up, peering over her spectacles at Opal. "You met our Matthias?"

She could still feel his lean strength under her arms as she clung tight during their ride, and a burn rose up her neck. Keeping her focus on the bread dough as she kneaded, she tried to maintain a casual tone. "He provided transportation for my journey back from the creek. Or rather, his horse did. 'Tis quite a fine animal. Have you seen it?"

She didn't usually prattle on so, but maybe the tumble of words would distract the matron from Opal's angst about the man.

"Ja. Karl is a fine steed. Good like the man."

Opal flipped the dough over and pressed the heels of her hands into the floury underside.

Mrs. S. seemed willing to let the subject drop, too. How wonderful that the woman knew how to appreciate the comfort of silence.

They worked that way for a good quarter hour before Mrs. S. straightened from the strudel she'd prepared and wiped her hands on a damp towel. "I'll go see what's keeping him."

"He's probably still settling his horse at the livery."

Mrs. S. murmured something as she left the room, but whether she spoke in English or German, her guttural accent made the word come out as an indecipherable growl.

Another quarter hour passed as Opal finished with the dough and separated it into pans to rise again, then mixed a batch of sweet rolls. Today being Wednesday, the mercantile owner's wife would expect a delivery before their evening meal. Most of the town had regular deliveries coordinated, mostly of the thirty-six loaves of bread they baked each morning, but also of the various other baked treats.

Mrs. S. had developed a thriving business for herself. It was enough to keep them both busy baking and Mr. S. scampering about town making deliveries. 'Twas a wonder the couple hadn't keeled over from exhaustion when it had been just the two of them trying to accomplish it all.

A noise sounded in the back of the house, and Opal watched the kitchen doorway as the Shumeisters' voices blended with a deeper male vibrato that must be Mr. Björk.

She pulled her focus back to her work and pressed out the dough in preparation for cutting lengths to roll. She shouldn't worry about the whereabouts of their guest. A strand of hair slipped loose from her braid, tickling her chin, so she pushed it behind her ear with her shoulder.

The voices became more distinct as the group neared the dining room.

"I'll stoke ze fire and start roasting ze meat. Go clean yourself up." Mrs. S.'s voice had taken on a motherly tone.

Mr. S. said something too quietly for her to decipher, then a moment later, his wife shuffled into the kitchen.

"Matthias brought us a deer for fresh meat." She held up a bundle large enough to fill both her hands. "He keeps us supplied, he does."

As Opal helped prepare and cook the meat, fresh juices made it seem like the venison had just been stripped from the carcass. Had he hunted it after she'd left him in the yard? Even if it had sat an hour or so, it seemed like the meat would have dried more than it had.

By the time they had dinner ready, the kitchen had grown warm with the savory aroma of jerked venison.

"Go call our menfolk to ze table." Mrs. S. used the back of her wrist to brush back a strand of wiry gray hair that had slipped from her kerchief. Juices from the meat shone from her hands from where she'd been slicing the roast into thick slabs.

Opal wiped her floury hands on her apron and moved to Mrs. S. "I'll finish that. You call them and sit down to enjoy your supper and our company." With any luck, she could stay busy in the kitchen and not have to sit at all. 'Twas not that she didn't enjoy the Shumeisters. She'd come to love them immensely in the several months she'd worked here. And Doctor Howard, their only regular boarder, was a good-hearted, fatherly man. Besides, his work kept him busy, so he often missed the evening meal and came home with exhaustion lines deepening the grooves in his face.

No, 'twas not the doctor or the Shumeisters she was hoping to avoid. Something about their newest guest unnerved her. Actually, most men unnerved her, but his effect held something unique.

Maybe 'twas the way a kind of virile manliness seemed to emanate from him. Or maybe 'twas the way the Shumeisters seemed to adore him. She wasn't jealous of their affections. Of course, she wasn't. After all, they'd known him much longer than she'd been working for these good people.

After setting out the dishes and food in the dining room, she was able to tuck herself away in the kitchen for a good part of the meal, scrubbing used pots and cleaning up from the day's baking.

The door between the kitchen and eating area opened, and Opal turned to see what Mrs. S. would need. Probably a refill of the spicy tea they liked to drink in the evenings.

But the blond head that peered through the doorway didn't belong to Mrs. Shumeister. The room shrunk as Matthias Björk carried the kettle in and placed it on the stove top. "I'm afraid we drank all the tea, but I'll brew some more." He glanced at her, his gaze taking in the soapy water that covered up to her elbows as she scrubbed the big pot.

"Aren't you going to come eat?" Innocent confusion puckered his brows, then melted away as his eyes narrowed. "I won't bite. Promise." He turned to the barrel of clean water, obviously knowing exactly where to find it, lifted the lid, and ladled out enough for a pot of tea. Then he reached for the canister of dried herbal leaves Mrs. S. had imported from a specialty retailer in Boston. 'Twas, it seemed to Opal, their only luxury.

She turned back to her work as Mr. Björk replaced the lid on the kettle. She listened for his heavy tread moving back to the dining room, but only the crackle of the fire in the cook stove greeted her straining ears. She turned her head slightly to view him from the corner of her eye.

He leaned against the wall near the cook stove, one foot cocked and arms crossed over his chest. He noticed her sideways glance and tipped the corner of his mouth. "Have you learned to appreciate tea at every meal yet?"

She turned away quickly so he wouldn't see the way his roguish look affected her. But the flip of her stomach was unnerving nonetheless.

Thankfully, he seemed oblivious. "You can't spend time around Mutti and Vatti without learning to like tea. *Dree is ostfreesenrecht.* Have you heard Vatti say that?"

Opal couldn't help turning to him as the image flashed through her mind of Mr. S. with a dainty mug in his hand, a twinkle in his faded blue eyes. "Three is their right." It pulled a smile from her just thinking about it. Both of them religiously drank three cups of tea at every sitting, as though their entrance into heaven depended on it.

Mr. Björk's mouth curved in a gentle smile, his gaze drifting into a memory. "They're good people, the Shumeisters. Best I've found."

19

Something about the wistfulness in his tone, or maybe the hint of longing in his eyes, made her look away. She should force her focus back onto her work before the burn in her throat grew into tears. She knew what 'twas like to feel that longing. That craving for a family. For someone to care.

Opal had it in her cousin Tori. And it seemed like she'd found it here with this quiet German couple. This haven they'd provided her, this safe place to live and be loved, 'twas a dream she'd never thought could come true.

But…oh, she had to stop thinking about this or she'd not be able to hold back her emotions. A warm drop slipped through her lashes and down her right cheek. She blinked the rest of the moisture back and stiffened her spine. The only way to hold the tears at bay was to change the topic of conversation.

"'Tis been how many months since you were here last? Five?" She scrubbed harder at a spot of burnt potato on the cast iron base of the pot.

"That's right. You were visiting family, I think?"

She nodded. "My cousin. She lives near her husband's family at a stage stop on the Oregon Trail. They're expecting an addition to their family in a few months." He probably didn't care about that last detail, but it slipped out anyway. Maybe because Tori's last letter still sat fresh in her mind. Maybe she could pen an answer tonight after the chores were finished.

"Do you have other family in the territories?"

20

How had they gotten onto this subject? The last thing she wanted to discuss with this Man of the Overpowering Presence was her family. Other than Tori, her father was her only living relative, and some days she wished she didn't have to claim him.

Despite his lack of attention during her growing up years, she never imagined Father wouldn't care when she completely disappeared from his life. He'd not come to find her after she and Tori had left home in the middle of the night. Not attempted to rescue her when his villainous steward chased after them. He didn't seem to care at all whether she was safe.

Yes, some days she'd rather be an orphan like Tori. That would be easier than fighting the sting of tears that still threatened every time she thought of her father's complete apathy.

Later that night, when all evening chores were finished, Opal still lingered in the quiet kitchen. This room had become her favorite, and even now the yeasty scents made the place feel warm and cozy.

Voices murmured from the other room where Mr. and Mrs. S. sat with Mr. Björk around the grand fireplace. She'd been invited to join them but begged off saying she was so exhausted, she planned to retire to her chamber soon.

And she would, after she wrote to Tori. She preferred the warmth of the kitchen to her room. With no hearths above stairs, the rooms tended to stay cold now that winter had come upon them. Especially after the sun disappeared each evening.

After gathering paper and pen from the corner cabinet, she pulled out a chair at the little work table and settled in.

Dearest Cousin,

Your letter made me smile, as always. How wonderful that you're feeling the baby move so much now. I can only imagine what 'tis like to feel the flutterings of new life growing inside. I can't wait to snuggle your tiny babe myself. Only a few more months now. I'll come right after Christmas so I'm sure to be there when your precious little one arrives to greet us.

Something interesting happened in Mountain Bluff today. Well, not actually in MB, but not far outside of town. Do you remember my telling you about the mountain man who provides meat for the Shumeisters? They speak of him with such affection, almost as if he's their son. He last came when I was visiting with you, but he came again today in a most startling way.

I had walked to a distant creek to gather willow bark and winter savory when he came galloping up on his massive white horse, almost like the knights of old.

A Mountain Christmas Romance

He and the horse attempted to jump over the creek but didn't realize I was kneeling beside the water until too late. The horse startled, and man and beast both ended up in the stream. Fortunately, neither was injured.

Opal nibbled the top of the pen. At least, she didn't think they were hurt. She'd checked the horse herself, but could Mr. Björk have been wounded and tried to conceal it? If so, at least he had the doctor here to consult.

If he would. He seemed like the type of wilderness man who would ignore his injuries in an attempt to conceal any weakness—maybe even to his own harm. But why was she even worried about this? He'd simply slipped off his horse while the animal fell into the creek. Mr. Björk was more likely to suffer from frostbite than a wound.

And he had mentioned that possibility. With wet boots, icy temperatures, and the sharp mountain wind, he may have sustained permanent damage on the long ride back.

She placed her pen on the table and started to rise, then stopped herself.

He was a grown man. He'd even had opportunity to speak to the doctor before the man retired to his chamber for the night. If Mr. Björk needed medical attention, he could seek it himself.

He wasn't her responsibility.

Chapter Three

*M*atthias stepped in through the back door the next morning with an armload of wood, the tune of a mountain birdsong on his lips. The aromas emanating from the kitchen were enough to make anybody sing—man or bird. No matter how much he traveled, he'd not found a cook in all the western territories who could make sourdough bread like Mutti Shumeister. And she had a loaf ready for breakfast each morning he was there.

After using his shoulder to push through the kitchen door, he took in the flurry of activity before depositing the load of oak logs he'd cut short enough to fit inside the cook stove's fire box.

Mutti sat at the table rolling some kind of thin pastry, and Miss Boyd worked at the taller counter.

"Hallo, Matthias. You are hungry, *ja*?" Only the twinkle in Mutti's eye gave evidence of her smile.

"I could eat ten loaves of your famous bread." He rested a hand on each of her fleshy shoulders, then leaned down to plant a solid kiss on her cheek.

"*Nein*, go on." She waved him off in the flustered way she usually responded to his affections.

He chuckled and patted her shoulder as he straightened. They did this same song and dance every time he came, and 'twas fun to see the red creep into her face as she pretended not to enjoy the attention.

"How can I help? I hope you saved a job so I can work for my food." He turned to scan the room, his gaze stalling on the lithe form of Miss Boyd as she wrapped bread loaves in a cloth bundle.

She'd pulled her blond hair into a braid, which hung almost the length of her back. A glorious length, and the tips looked feathery soft where they flared out from the ribbon she'd used to fasten the end.

"You can make ze deliveries zis morning." Mutti waved to the cloth bundles Miss Boyd had already prepared.

He nodded and moved to the packages next to Miss Boyd. A light scent of apples laced with the yeasty flavor of the bread, and their combined aroma filled his senses enough to make him lightheaded. Maybe he was just hungry, but the woman's nearness seemed to overpower his every thought.

Miss Boyd tapped the bundles as she instructed him. "This goes to the leather shop. This to Mr. Williams. And these to the mercantile. Oh, and we have some for Mr. Lefton at the livery, too."

Matthias cringed. Not that man.

"Nein." Mutti's sharp call made them both look up. "Not the livery. Gunther will deliver that one. Only the others."

Matthias didn't look at the maiden beside him as he reached for the bundles. He hated the way the Shumeisters tried to shield him from that oaf. But they didn't want trouble, and as long as Matthias stayed under their roof, he would abide by their strictures. Besides, the man was their paying customer, and he couldn't jeopardize that income.

The burn of Miss Boyd's stare heated his face, but he ignored it as he gathered the packages and turned toward the door.

Opal and Mrs. S. had breakfast ready by the time Mr. Björk returned from his deliveries. Mr. S had shuffled out not long after the younger man with the delivery to Mr. Lefton at the town stable. It still made no sense why Mr. Björk couldn't have taken it all, but when she questioned Mrs. S, the older woman had only shrugged. She wasn't usually talkative, but when she didn't want to answer a question, it was impossible to get a word from her.

Mr. Björk sat at the table with the doctor, sipping coffee while the older man filled him in on recent events around town. Doctor Howard worked his way through a plate of meats, cheese, and bread slathered with blackberry preserves, but Matthias hadn't loaded anything on his dish. It appeared he planned to wait until Mr. S. returned to break his fast, a thoughtfulness the older man would appreciate.

Opal was just bringing the coffee pot to refill their mugs when the front door crashed open. "Doc. Come quick."

Little Benjamin from the mercantile staggered into the room, panting and gripping his side. This wasn't the first time he'd come running for the doctor, and his presence always tightened a knot in Opal's stomach.

Doctor Howard wiped his mouth with a serviette as he rose from the table. "What is it, Ben?"

The boy glanced at Opal, then turned back to the doctor. "Mr. Shumeister. He got knocked down by Big Dan at the livery an' he's hurt bad."

Opal's foot snagged in the carpet, and she stumbled forward to the table. Grabbing the edge, she righted herself and set the coffee pot onto its surface with a clatter. The image of the big bay stallion at the livery filled her mind's eye. The stallion that had a reputation for wildness. What had Mr. S. been doing close enough to the animal to be knocked down?

She headed for the door and Benjamin as the others gathered around the boy. "How badly is he injured?"

"Don't know for sure. He was holdin' his arm an' groanin', so Mr. Lefton sent me runnin' to get you."

Opal's pulse thundered as they all stamped out the door and down the street, but her skirts slowed her so much that Mr. Björk and the doctor quickly outpaced her. Mrs. S.

moved even slower, and Opal finally pulled them both to a walk as the older woman panted.

She threaded her arm through Mrs. S.'s. "I'm sure he's fine." At least she prayed he was. Mr. Shumeister wasn't a young man, and his bones were likely more fragile than they'd once been.

A cluster of figures had gathered in the street ahead, and the sight coiled the ball of dread even tighter in her stomach. She wanted to run to them, but Mrs. S. was leaning heavily on her arm now, and the older woman needed her more than the men did.

She patted the woman's hand. "I'm sure he'll be fine. The doctor's with him now."

Before they reached the group, people were beginning to disperse. Three figures rose from the street and limped toward them. They were still a hundred feet away, but from their profiles, it was easy to see the man in the middle was the hunched form of Mr. Shumeister. The doctor and Mr. Björk flanked him, and the sight of all three walking eased the knot in Opal's stomach.

"My Gunther." Mrs. S. pulled away from Opal, gripped her skirts, and broke into a run again.

Opal did the same, but more to be there for Mrs. S. than anything else. The older woman didn't get around as well as someone half her age, and this fright couldn't be good for her nerves or her heart. If anything happened to either of the Shumeisters...the thought was too awful to even consider.

28

When they reached the men, Mrs. S. took Matthias Björk's place at her husband's side, murmuring in what must have been German. Opal looked to Doctor Howard, the knot in her throat choking off her breathing as she scanned his face for some sign of how bad it was.

The doctor met her gaze. "I think his arm's broken, but there doesn't seem to be more. We'll get him home to splint it."

Only a broken arm. She nodded, letting all the fear trapped inside leak out in a long breath. She turned on unsteady legs as the others started back toward the boardinghouse. With Mr. S. flanked by his wife and doctor, she and Mr. Björk took places behind them.

It seemed strange to walk beside the man, and she fought a wave of uneasiness. Especially since he might be considered the cause of Mr. S.'s injury, in a roundabout way. After all, if Björk had taken the bread to the livery, Mr. S. wouldn't have been in that dangerous place when the horse went struck out. And maybe this was her chance to ask why. "Mr. Björk, why did Mr. S. deliver the loaves to the livery instead of you? Why didn't Mrs. S. want you to go?"

He was silent as they walked. The pace was more of a stroll really, as the trio ahead moved at a turtle's speed. "Call me Matthias."

She glanced at him. "Beg pardon?"

Something flexed in his jaw. "Everyone calls me Matthias. I'd prefer you do the same."

29

"Are you avoiding my question?" She couldn't fathom what gave her the boldness to confront him, other than the fact that his response irked her.

A corner of his mouth twitched. "I have no idea why Lefton dislikes me, but 'tis a fact. It bothers Mrs. S. when we get in a row, so I oblige her and stay away from the place." He slid a glance at her. "I can't be running off the paying customers."

Then a sadness entered his eyes that gave hint of his regret. "I wish I'd gone today, though. A broken arm causes a powerful pain."

"You sound as though you've experienced it."

His eyes narrowed. "I've done my share of impulsive antics."

The words gave her pause. "You mean like riding pell-mell through the mountains with a lady clinging to the back of your horse?" She nibbled the inside of her lip. She wasn't normally so outspoken, but something about this man raised her dander. Or perhaps Tori had finally rubbed off on her.

"At least no one broke her arm during that ride."

Thankfully, they'd reached the boardinghouse door, so she was saved a response. Probably a good thing, because she had nothing kind to retort.

Over the next few days, Opal worked to settle in to the new routine of the household. The doctor had splinted Mr. S.'s arm and bound it tight to his chest. He spent much of his time in the overstuffed chair by the large hearth, reading or sleeping. When he wasn't entertaining visitors from around town, that was. The Shumeisters were such good people, and that fact wasn't hidden from neighbors, despite the couple's quiet ways and heavy German accents.

Mrs. S. rarely left her husband's side unless he was sleeping, which was as it should be. And the extra work made it easier for Opal to hide herself in the kitchen or the backyard, away from the steady stream of visitors.

Matthias seemed to keep busy, too, taking over all of Mr. S.'s responsibilities around the place. Which meant she saw him throughout each day when he restocked her wood supply or carried in fresh water. And, of course, at every meal.

She would have thought these frequent interactions would make her immune to the strength of his presence. But still, each time he walked into the room, her senses came alive. She could feel his every movement, whether she had her back turned to him or not. And her skin would almost tingle when he turned those sharp green eyes on her.

What was it about him that seemed to steal the air from the room? It must be the aura of wildness he emanated, with those broad shoulders and the way his blond hair was just long enough to curl at the nape of his neck. Not to mention the stubble that glittered on his face by the end of each day.

Which was another thing that surprised her. She would have expected a mountain man to let his beard grow

31

shaggy, especially during the winter months. Yet Matthias appeared to shave each day.

"Your thoughts are deep."

Opal caught her breath as she turned from the laundry basin to see Mrs. S. standing behind her, squinting against the late morning sun. She tried to smile, but 'twas hard to force her mind to break through the web of thoughts. "Washing makes for good thinking."

Mrs. S. studied her, and Opal turned back to the shirt she was scrubbing on the washboard. "How is Mr. S. this morning?"

"Sleeping. His pain is better now. I think 'tis time I resume my work."

Opal glanced at her. "I'm taking care of things. You should be there when he needs you. Don't worry about the baking, I'll let you know if I need help." She'd spent an early morning in the kitchen, then several more hours after breakfast, and finally escaped outside with the laundry to soak up a few rays of the winter sunshine.

"Nein. You are almost done with ze clothes. I pack lunch for you to take with Matthias. Go for a ride and let him show you ze fountains of water."

"What? No." Mrs. S. was sending them out for a picnic? She straightened and wrung out the shirt, then looked around at her work. This was the last of the clothing she'd brought outside, but she could probably find more to wash if she looked for it. It shouldn't be hard to convince the woman she was too busy to go for a joyride.

Mrs. S. reached for the satchel of clean, wet clothes. With the weather hovering so cold outside, they usually hung laundry to dry in the solarium, a room near the back of the house encased in wax paper windows so they could grow herbs and seasonings through the winter months.

"Let me carry those." Opal reached to take the bundle from the woman's arms, exchanging it for the washboard and bar of soap—a lighter load.

Mrs. S. accepted the items and turned with Opal toward the house. "Matthias will empty the wash bucket, and I will hang zese clothes while you go to gather your horse."

Opal let out a huff. So many things wrong with this picture. If she were going for a ride with Matthias, why couldn't he retrieve Butter from the livery like a gentleman normally would? Why must he be so protected from Mr. Lefton? Maybe now was the time to ask. "Mrs. S., what happened between Matthias and Mr. Lefton? Why do we keep them apart?"

The woman grunted as they reached the back door. "It is God's business, and He's taking care of it. Put ze clothes in the sun room and go prepare for your ride."

Argh. Opal wanted to release a frustrated grunt, but knew better than to be so disrespectful. What did Mrs. S. mean, *God's business*? And why was she so insistent that Opal go on this outing?

She'd been working long hours lately, and an afternoon away *would* be a blessed relief. But could she leave the Shumeisters for so long? And did she really want to spend that much time with Matthias? She wasn't concerned about him being dishonorable. At least, she didn't think so. After watching him with Mr. and Mrs. S., it seemed he had a good heart. But his presence was distracting. Could she spend an afternoon with him and not be affected to the edge of her sanity?

Chapter Four

*D*espite Opal's objections, a half hour later she was mounted on Butter and following Matthias's broad shoulders as he and his gelding led them down the mountain trail. She shouldn't be leaving all the chores for Mrs. S., but maybe a short outing would be all right.

They rode in quiet for a while, which gave her the chance to soak in the brisk air and the sounds of nature. The trail wound through forests of evergreens, then onto open rocky ground and around clusters of giant boulders and buttes. The wild beauty of this land never ceased to invigorate her, weaving through her chest so that all her struggles seemed to melt away.

Matthias pointed out some of the landmarks they passed, including the deer path down the mountain that crossed their own trail. "That's where I caught the buck I brought to Mutti this time. Whenever I'm in need of fresh meat, one of these trails is the surest way to find game."

"Do you travel this way often?"

35

He nodded. "Almost every trip. This is the easiest way north from Mountain Bluff."

"What made you become a mountain man?" She hadn't planned to be so nosy, but mystery seemed to shroud him, and something inside her craved to know more. Not just to know *about* him, but to know *him*. What caused Matthias to choose this life over that of a miller, or blacksmith, or storekeeper?

He was silent for a long moment as the trail wound downward. Perhaps she had pushed too far, asking questions that were none of her business.

But at last he spoke. "I come from a long line of Vikings." He turned back to look at her. "Do you know what a Viking is?"

Of course, she'd heard of Vikings. What had she learned from her historical studies at the Boiling Springs School for Girls? "They were marauders of old, weren't they? From Norway?" That would explain his fair hair and those piercing green eyes.

He nodded. "And other Scandinavian nations. My people came from Iceland after the Mist Hardships in the seventeen hundreds."

"Mist Hardships?" A sudden longing pressed in her chest. What must it be like to know where one's ancestors had lived over a hundred years before?

"A volcano erupted in the Laki mountains, spewing lava and poisonous mist for eight months. It killed most of the

36

animals and plants, and the famine afterwards starved a great many people. Those who could escaped."

She stared at him, trying to absorb the extent of the damage he described. "And your family came to America."

"I can remember my mum saying how these mountains are so much like those in Iceland. Even the geysers are the same."

"What is that?" He spoke so casually about having come from a foreign land, one she'd barely heard of and couldn't have placed on a map. Maybe 'twas not so different than the fact that her family had once lived in England. Although a country named *Iceland* sounded so much more exciting than plain old England.

"I'll explain the geysers when we arrive." He glanced over his shoulder, and the mischievous tilt of his mouth made her stomach flip. Where exactly was he taking her?

They rode in silence a few minutes longer as the horses picked their way down a trail that edged around the base of a rocky butte. She tried to imagine a young tow-headed boy scampering through these mountains with his fair-haired parents. 'Twas hard to think of the strapping man sitting atop the gray steed in front of her as ever having been small and wiry.

"So what about you, Miss Boyd? Why did you become a baker?"

She glanced up as his question pulled her from her imaginings. "I..." She'd have to tread cautiously to sidestep the question without revealing what had truly driven her to this place of safety. "My cousin and I came to the Wyoming Territory to meet her correspondence partner, whom she happened to marry." She pinched back a grin at the memories. "Before he convinced Tori to marry him, Ezra was trying to secure work for us. He met the Shumeisters, and they agreed to take us on, but not long after that, Tori succumbed to his charms." An image of her cousin's radiant smile on her wedding day flashed through her mind. That was the day that changed both their lives, mostly for the good.

"But you still decided to come work for Mutti and Vatti?"

She nodded. "Why do you call them that? Those names—they aren't their German names, are they?"

He flicked another glance over his shoulder. "It means mum and dad in German. The first time I met them, I was half-dead from some type of winter sickness. Between the doc and Mutti, they nursed me back to health, then Vatti read to me from his Bible for hours on end. By the time winter was over and I'd recovered enough to head back into the mountain country, they liked to call me their new son. They seemed to appreciate when I teased them with the German names, so I just kept on."

His voice had dipped low and soft, laced with a tenderness that made her chest ache. "They're good people. I try to do what I can to help them."

She swallowed the lump in her throat. "They love you, and I know they appreciate the meat you bring them. I think Mrs. S. wishes you'd stay longer on your visits, though."

He shrugged. "'Tis about time I head back out again."

The casual words felt like a slap, as though he were intentionally trying to show that he didn't care what the Shumeisters wanted. Had she imagined the tenderness in his tone only moments before?

Matthias didn't speak again for a long time, maybe close to an hour. Maybe 'twas the silence, or maybe the beauty of their surroundings, the mix of mountain wilderness with the rich color of the evergreens, but her irritation with the man seemed to ebb away. It didn't matter what he said or did. She was here to simply enjoy the spectacular scenery.

Matthias looked back at her. "We're not far now."

"Not far from what?"

The eager grin marking his face made it easier to imagine him as that little blond boy she'd tried to picture before. He didn't answer, just smiled and turned back to the trail as his horse rounded a curve in the trees.

The path opened into a somewhat level area with a few spots of winter-brown grass interspersed with rocks of the same color. The bedrock had been crushed into loose pebbles in some areas, and in other spots, it sank into basins where water had pooled.

"Is this what we came to see?" The place was different from the rougher terrain they'd traveled so far, but it wasn't particularly lovely or awe-inspiring.

"Sort of." He reined his gelding around a pool of dark water. "We'll eat lunch here and wait for a spout."

Maybe she'd misunderstood that last word. Perhaps this was a special gathering place for deer or other wildlife, which would make sense with all the shallow water pools for drinking.

He led them to the far side of the clearing where the land sloped in a gradual incline, away from the water. When he dismounted, she did the same and reached for the bundle of food Mrs. S. had secured behind her saddle.

Matthias produced a canteen and a blanket for them to sit on, then he settled the horses in a grassy area to graze.

Every nerve in her came alive as he approached the blanket where she'd knelt and was setting out the foodstuffs. What was it about his presence that affected her so? Maybe 'twas the fact that she shouldn't trust him. Like most men she'd known.

He reached for the food pack and unrolled a loaf of bread, then extracted his knife from the sheath at his waist. She slid a glance at him as he sliced the bread while she did the same with the cheese.

He picked up one of the cloths that had wrapped the food, then positioned cheese on two slices of bread and laid the bundle beside her. "Here you go." He moved the canteen closer. "Mutti sent tea, even though I told her water would be sufficient. She always loves too much."

As an affectionate expression crossed his face, she couldn't help the way her heart softened a little more. Maybe she'd misunderstood his harsh words from before. Or maybe she'd read too much into them. "Thank you."

She took her first bite, savoring the blend of rich smoked cheese and yeasty sourdough. The stiffness in her shoulders eased out as the food and the clear mountain air worked their magic.

"Look. I think one is starting."

She turned at Matthias's words, then let her gaze follow the reach of his finger to one of the larger pools about thirty feet from them. The water's surface had begun to bubble. "What is that?"

But as she watched, the bubbles began to rise higher in one particular spot, until they lifted over a foot high into a sort of fountain.

She glanced at Matthias to catch his expression. He'd been watching the water, but now turned to her with a sparkle in his eyes.

"Have you seen this before?"

He nodded. "Watch." His focus tracked back to the pool.

The fountain rose higher, then with a snapping sound, the water surged upward. Ten feet. Twelve feet.

She sucked in a breath. *Magnificent.*

Mist cloaked the air as the plume of water surged and ebbed in a powerful dance. "What did you say that's called?" She couldn't take her gaze from the spectacle before them.

"A geyser." The soft reverence in his tone matched the feeling that resonated in her chest.

A glimmer caught her attention, and she glanced to the left where a shimmering arc of color rose into the gray-blue winter sky. She reached for Matthias's arm and gripped it. "A rainbow."

"Nice." His voice came out a low rumble, and she could only sit mesmerized.

This was truly amazing. One couldn't see such miracles in nature without knowing for certain God cared. She hadn't always believed, but living with Mr. and Mrs. S., 'twas impossible not to see and feel their unwavering faith in His love and daily provision.

As the mist from the spray caressed her skin, she raised her face to the heavens and let her eyes drift shut. *For as the heaven is high above the earth, so great is his mercy toward them that fear him.* She'd read the verse just that morning, and it brought another surge of love, which cloaked her with a sense of fullness and peace she couldn't remember ever having felt before.

After another moment reveling in the feeling, quiet settled over her. Opening her eyes, she looked toward the geyser, but the fountain had lowered back to about a foot high. Slowly, it faded until only bubbles and foam gathered on the water's surface.

She inhaled a deep breath, trying to pull her raw emotions back to a semblance of control. A glance at Matthias showed he was watching her, so she summoned a smile. "Is that what we came to see?"

He nodded, his eyes shimmering. "What did you think?"

She couldn't put these overflowing feelings into words if she tried. So, she focused on one of his earlier comments. "You said they have geysers in Iceland?"

"Yes."

"I think Iceland must be a glimpse of heaven."

He raised his brows. "A land named Iceland? It sounds cold to me."

She couldn't help a real smile. "With mountains like these and magnificent acts of God like we just saw, I can't imagine a better place."

Matthias landed a solid blow on the head of the nail, sinking it deep into the wood planks at the rear corner of the boardinghouse. He still had two more sides to go before he finished resetting the loose nails in the building's exterior.

This project seemed to be dragging as slowly as the last five days had since he'd taken Opal to see the geyser. He had to get this finished though. Now that Vatti was feeling better and on his feet again, he'd freed him up to take care of the repairs and the harder work that needed to be done around the place.

And the sooner he finished, the sooner he could leave.

He hadn't realized how close he was getting to these people until Opal's comments during their ride. He'd come to care too much for Mutti and Vatti. And they for him. That care could only bring them pain and suffering.

It had already started with Vatti being injured making the delivery that Matthias should have handled, and would have if it hadn't been for that crazed livery owner and his unfounded hatred. It still made no sense why the man held such a vendetta against him. That first day Matthias rode into town and tried to board Karl in a stall, Lefton chased him away with a pitchfork, threatening to replace it with a rifle.

The man was obviously a lunatic, but Matthias shouldn't have cowered and allowed Vatti to go on that delivery. 'Twas just one more time his poor decisions had brought pain and hardship to someone he cared about.

And now he'd best get out of town before someone else got hurt.

He landed another blow, but the nail curved like it had weakened from too much time in the harsh weather. He pulled a newly forged nail from his coat pocket and fit it beside the older piece. This one drove straight and smooth, the nail head seating cleanly in the wood with only two strikes.

"Matthias?"

He stiffened, then slowly stood and looked to the back door. The pretty face that accompanied that delicate voice tightened his chest like it had every time he'd seen Opal since their ride.

That was another reason why he needed to leave. His body reacted far too strongly to this woman. He probably shouldn't have taken her on the picnic, but Mutti had been so insistent, and she rarely asked for anything.

He'd kept his distance fairly well for the first half of the outing. Until the geyser had spouted and she'd been so caught up in the sight that her face practically glowed. Like the angel she was.

Which made her far too special for a rough mountain Viking like him.

"Matthias, Darrel just brought a telegram for you."

A telegram. The moment the words started to register, he dropped his hammer and strode toward her. "Who sent it?"

She glanced at the paper folded in her hand. "I haven't opened it. Should I have?"

He reached her and extended his hand to take it. "No. Sorry. That's fine." The surge of energy pulsing through his veins made his fingers shake, so he snatched the paper and turned away. Would this be good news? He'd sent inquiries to several more towns last week, extending his search for Alanna northward.

He fumbled with the edges and unfolded the note. In small, concise script, the message stared up at him.

Responding to your inquiry, stop. Nilsen family in Jackson until four years ago, stop. Moved north, stop.

Matthias stared at the paper as the letters swirled in his vision. *Nilsen family in Jackson.* He'd found a trace of them. This must be his father's aunt and uncle—and Alanna. At least, God willing, Alanna would still be with them. *Let her be alive and well.*

He spun back around, his mind racing through all the supplies he'd need to gather before heading out.

Opal stood just outside the doorway, watching him.

"I have to go."

She tilted her head, her honey-colored brows lowering as if she were trying to make sense of him. "Go where?"

"To find my sister." His bedroll was packed, but he'd need to gather enough food to keep him for several days. The sky had simmered with dark clouds all morning, which meant the grass would be covered with snow for the next few days, and he'd need to take oats for Karl. Just as well. He'd rather not take the time to let the animal graze.

He moved to go around Opal, and she stepped aside out of the doorway.

"You're leaving town?"

He glanced over his shoulder. "I have to." The weather may not be ideal for traveling, especially through the mountains, but this was the first time he'd found a confirmed residence. He had to check into it.

Chapter Five

earest Opal,

A knight on his charger? Oh, cousin, this mountain man sounds intriguing. If the Shumeisters think so highly of him, he must be a man of good character. We've not met many of those, especially growing up at Riverdale. But I can assure you, such men do exist. My Ezra is the best of them.

Has your mountain man been staying at the boardinghouse with you? Do write and tell me what he looks like. Is he tall? Are his features dark or fair? What is the horse's name?

I miss you, Opal. I miss our days riding together back in Riverdale. Ezra won't let me ride horseback at all anymore, now that my condition is so advanced. I even offered to sit side-saddle (which you know I detest), but he's concerned the horse might throw me and injure the baby. I pretended to be frustrated, and I am a little, but honestly, it's nice to feel so protected. I hope you have found that same protection with Mr. and Mrs. S.

I look forward to your next letter, and please make sure to be forthcoming with details about Mr. Björk.

Your loving cousin,
Tori

Opal stared at the letter, fighting the churn of emotions in her chest. Tori had jumped to conclusions about her feelings for Matthias.

She scanned the note again. Tori hadn't actually asked whether she liked the man, just assumed it. She'd commented about the potential for his good character. From everything Opal had seen, Matthias did seem to be a man of strong moral conduct—excluding that one comment during their ride, which she must have misunderstood.

He'd spent the last two weeks helping Mr. and Mrs. S., doing everything from running errands to making repairs to chopping firewood. He brought them meat and helped provide in other areas, too. And the way his expression softened when he planted a peck on Mrs. S.'s cheek was enough to make any girl swoon. Even Mrs. S. seemed befuddled each time.

The only thing that remained at odds with the picture her mind created of the man was Mr. Lefton's hatred toward him. The livery owner seemed like a decent fellow, although she'd never spent much time in his presence. But Matthias must have done something to incite such a violent reaction. He'd said he didn't know why the man hated him, but surely he must have some idea.

So many questions.

Mrs. S. marched into the kitchen with her usual brusque efficiency. "We have a new boarder. I put him in the blue room."

Opal laid the letter on the table and pushed to her feet. "How long is he staying?" They didn't often have boarders, since Mountain Bluff wasn't on a main thoroughfare. She tried to keep the empty rooms clean, though. "I'll take up a pitcher of water. Is there anything else he needs?"

Mrs. S. waved the question away. "Nein, only warm food to fill his belly. I'll make venison gulasch."

Opal pulled the spare pitcher from a shelf and filled it from the clean water barrel. "What's his name?"

"Elias Gultcher. He does...what you call it...mining. Staying a few weeks, he say."

A miner. She made her way out the kitchen door, through the dining room, and up the stairs. She'd heard of several mines to the south, and the men she'd met who worked them had all been dirty and careworn. She would need to be on her guard around the man.

Down the hall to the right, she stopped at the second door and gave a sturdy tap with her knuckle.

"It's not locked." A rough male voice sounded from the other side.

Did that mean open the door? She reached for the handle and pushed it open a crack. "I brought water for your basin, Mr. Gultcher."

"Bring it in."

She peered around the door and caught sight of a man standing by the window, his back to her. "Should I leave it here by the door?" There wasn't a table here, so she'd have to set it on the floor.

"Put it with the basin." He still didn't turn to look at her, but his voice held a decided tone of command, as though he were directing a servant. Or perhaps a slave, considering the edge of condescension.

"Yes, sir." Maybe she shouldn't acquiesce so quickly, but the words came too naturally. And besides, he'd spent good coin to stay here. And she was a paid employee, which could perhaps be considered not much better than a servant.

She stepped into the room, scooting quickly to the washbasin. He turned to look at her, but she ignored him. *Lord, let him stay over there.* She put the pitcher beside the basin as the prickle of his gaze warmed her neck.

Summoning her courage, she turned to face him. "Dinner will be ready in about an hour. Do you need anything else?"

He wasn't as haggard as she'd expected. Almost middle-aged with only a few lines around his eyes and a thick brown beard covering the lower half of his face.

But 'twas the way he looked at her that made her want to inch backward. That same glimmer of lust in his eyes she'd seen too many times from her father's steward at Riverdale. Even though Tori had borne the brunt of that man's improper advances, the way this miner looked at her now brought back that surge of fear in a smothering wave.

She stepped toward the door as her pulse picked up speed. "If you need anything else, just call to the kitchen." Or maybe Mr. Shumeister would be in the sitting area to assist the man.

She slipped through the door, then pulled it closed and took long strides to the stairs. Her knees almost buckled as she descended, but she clung to the rail for support.

Her safe haven had just become dangerous.

The next night, Opal dawdled outside when she took the bucket of dirty dishwater to dump it in the woods at the edge of the backyard. Mr. Gultcher had been sitting with Mr. S. at the dining table, recounting stories of his glory days in mining. Who knew whether half the stories were true? Mr. S. seemed somewhat entertained, but the way Gultcher slid his gaze over her figure every time she walked through the room made the hairs on the back of her neck stand on end.

She pulled her coat tighter around her shoulders as she scanned the yard, her gaze wandering toward the trail Matthias had traveled when he left. It'd been two weeks since he'd received the telegram. From what he said, he should have arrived in Jackson by now. Had he found good news? Maybe someone who knew where his sister had gone? The yearning in his eyes had been mixed with determination as he'd mounted his horse and nodded at her and Mrs. S. before riding away.

A whine sounded behind her, and Opal spun, taking a few steps away from the woods. She strained to see in the darkness. With the moon almost full, she'd not brought a lantern. What kind of animal made a whimper like that? She should probably go inside in case it was dangerous, but her curiosity wouldn't let her leave.

A rustle sounded in the leaves to her left, and a pale-yellow form emerged from the trees. A dog? She tensed, preparing to run if it seemed aggressive.

Its tail curled up over its body and fanned back and forth, but as it stepped forward, the animal seemed to be limping.

"Hey, there." She leaned down and extended her hand. "Are you hurt, fella?"

The dog whined again and slunk closer, still wagging its tail in a steady rhythm.

"Let's see what's wrong with you."

When the animal crept close enough, she stroked its head, her hand catching on leaves and sticks tangled in the hair. "Why don't you come to the house so I can get a lantern? Maybe we have some scraps you'd like." She slid her hand down its back, feeling the bony spine and protruding ribs. It didn't seem like the animal belonged to anyone, or if it did, that person should be tarred and feathered for neglecting it.

She eased upright and turned toward the house. "Come, boy. Let's go eat."

The dog stayed at the back door while she went inside to gather a lantern, food, and the medicine basket. When she stepped back out, it wagged its tail in greeting.

"You are a sweet boy, aren't you?" She sank down to sit on the stoop next to the animal. And when she stroked its head, the dog rolled onto its side, giving her an affectionate gaze. "My, goodness." What a sweetie. And yes, the dog did appear to be of the male persuasion.

She pulled a wheat roll from her coat pocket and tore off a chunk. The dog jumped to its feet and nosed forward. The moment she placed the food on the ground, it snapped the bread in a single bite, not even taking time to chew.

"Ho, there. Hungry?" She tore another chunk and dropped it, jerking her hand back as the dog repeated its snap-and-swallow routine. Within a minute, it had eaten both rolls she'd brought, even though she'd separated the bread into small bites.

She held up the lantern. "I'll get more food in a moment, but let's see if you're hurt." The dog's coat seemed a dirty yellow in the glow of the light. No obvious injury presented itself, just the rough, neglected look of a pet forced to fend for itself. Had its owner died? Or maybe they'd somehow become separated in the mountains.

53

Stroking its neck, she continued sliding her fingers down first one front leg, then the other.

The dog yelped when she reached its right paw, then jerked away from her, pulling the foot from her grasp.

"Poor dear." She held out her hand to coax the animal forward again. With a wary look, it approached, and she wrapped her arm around its big golden frame while examining the paw. A glance at the underside made the problem quite clear—a gash along the large center pad. Dirt coated the cut, clinging to what appeared to be pus oozing from the wound.

The dog wiggled as she examined the injury, so she paused to stroke its head again. "I think I'm going to need help to tend this."

Dare she take him inside? Mrs. S. had never mentioned animals, at least not live ones. But she possessed such a generous heart toward people, surely the woman wouldn't mind if she brought the dog inside so they could clean and bandage its paw.

Pushing to her feet, she gathered her supplies and patted her leg. "Come, boy."

The dog followed her into the house, and she took him into the solarium where she could close the door. After leaving the animal there, she found Mrs. S. exiting the kitchen. Mr. Gultcher's gaze burned her cheeks as she stepped into the dining room, but she ignored him. "Mrs. Shumeister, could I beg your assistance for a moment?"

"Of course." The woman followed her down the hallway.

Opal paused at the door to the solarium. "I found something outside that needs our help. I hope you don't mind."

"Ja, of course."

With her lip in her teeth, Opal pushed open the door. The dog met them inside, wagging its tail in an off-kilter jig as it tried not to put weight on the injured paw.

"Ooh." Mrs. S. bent and reached for the pup, who came forward to lick her hand.

"He has a gash on his right front paw that needs to be cleaned and bandaged. It pains him sorely, so would best be done with two people."

"Ja, of course."

Mrs. S. settled in to doctor the wound while Opal held the dog. He alternated between licking her hand and whimpering as she held him tight and stroked behind his ear. His body was so warm, it made her want to snuggle him in a hug for the rest of the night. What was it about animals that made them so easy to love?

Finally, Mrs. S. leaned back. "There. We should keep him in the house until it heals."

"Can we? He can stay in my room where he won't be in the way."

Mrs. S. studied her for a long moment. "Ja, all right." Then she pushed to her feet with a heavy grunt.

Opal pressed her cheek against the dog's head, and he returned the hug by twisting to lick her chin. She couldn't help a giggle as she pulled back.

"Now we need to find a name for you."

Chapter Six

harmer's tail thumped on the kitchen's wooden floor, blending with the crackle of the fire in the woodstove and the scraping of her biscuit cutter against the counter. These late morning moments in the kitchen always seeped in and soothed her nerves, letting her mind refocus on the things that mattered.

Like the verses she'd been committing to memory in Psalm. *I have set the Lord always before me: because he is at my right hand, I shall not be moved. Therefore my heart is glad, and my glory rejoiceth: my flesh also shall rest in hope.*

Had Tori also found the place where her heart was glad? Of course, having a husband who loved her and a baby on the way probably helped with that happiness. But did Tori also fully understand this joy that stirred in Opal's soul when she focused on the Lord?

Fitting the round dough circles in a row on the pan, she let a song find her lips. No words, just a jaunty rhythm that came to her in a hum.

57

Beside her, Charmer raised his head and stared at the door. She stilled her song so she could listen.

Boot thuds sounded in the dining room, spurring her heartbeat into a quicker pace. That wasn't Mr. S.'s gentle tread, but maybe the doctor? The heavy thumps had to be from a man. Mr. Gultcher should be out mining, or whatever it was he spent his daylight hours doing.

Yet something about the sound raised the fine hairs on the back of her neck. The door eased open, as though the man entering were trying not to disturb anyone inside—or maybe sneak up on them.

A face edged around the door wearing that dark beard that seemed to press down on her chest so that all her air fled. When he caught sight of her, something flashed across his expression. Only for a moment, but 'twas enough to light fear in her gut as that beard split to display brownish teeth in what he must have meant to be a smile.

Wiping her hands on a cloth she eased back a step. "Mr. Gultcher. I didn't expect you back this early in the day." He must not have gone mining. Oh, heavens. She hadn't been prepared to avoid him. "Do you need something?" The sooner she got him out of the kitchen, the better.

"'Nother cup o' coffee. An' whatever's smellin' up the place so good."

She stiffened. Why did his tone always make her feel like a scullery maid? The lowest of the staff. She raised her chin, affecting the look Tori always used when she wanted to ward off attention. "You're likely smelling the rolls cooking,

58

but they've already been promised to Mr. Lefton. We'll have cold sandwiches for luncheon in a couple hours."

She turned back to her biscuit dough and pressed the tin circle in a flattened section. If she ignored him, perhaps he would leave. Her words echoed in her ears, scalding her with their rudeness. Yet the sound of his breathing gradually overpowered all other noise. Had he stepped closer? She'd not heard his footsteps.

And then, the thump of a boot heel striking the floor filled the room, bringing all her senses to life. Another thump. Closer?

She couldn't stop herself from glancing over her shoulder to check.

The sight made her breath still in her chest. He was *definitely* closer, and moving toward her with a leer on his face that gave no doubt of his intentions.

She stepped backward, glancing behind her for a way of escape. Only the pantry, but maybe she could get in there and bar the door. There was no lock installed for the room, and certainly not from the inside.

Her gaze slid around the kitchen. Maybe she could dash around him. This area wasn't very wide, so he could probably reach his grubby paws and grab her. But maybe if she threw something at him. Distracted him.

"Maybe I'll have something else then, if you're not gonna feed me." He advanced another step, looming larger before her.

She backed up, darting a glance at the counter. What could she throw to distract him? She'd already stepped too far away from the rolling pin and knives. The only things within easy reach were her cloth and a mound of bread dough she'd set aside to let rise. Could she throw the dough so it covered his eyes?

"Since there's no one here to object, maybe I'll just get my fill of you." He moved forward again. "I've seen the way you look at me. You want it as much as I do."

How had she looked at him? Not at all except in fear and revulsion. What had she done that he could possibly confuse for wanting? "No. I don't." She shook her head. "I didn't mean to confuse you. I don't want anything from you. Please, leave me alone."

He was almost close enough to grab her now, but if she stepped back, she wouldn't be able to reach the bread dough. And there was nothing else on the length of the counter. Nothing. Why had she kept the place so clean?

"I know you're just being a modest little chit. You want it as much as I do." He stepped nearer, close enough now that he could reach out and grab her.

Fear clawed in her chest, ripping at her lungs so she couldn't draw breath. "No. Please."

She tensed to reach for the dough. She'd have to do it all in one quick motion, for surprise would be her only advantage.

A growl sounded from somewhere out of her vision. *Charmer.*

60

Gultcher took his focus off her to look at the animal. Now was the time. She had to act before he hurt Charmer, too.

Ripping the cloth cover from the rising mound, she grabbed the slippery dough and hurled it at the man's eyes.

He stumbled back, and she darted to the side, out of reach of those flailing arms. But he grabbed her wrist, jerking her hard as he scrambled for his balance.

A bark sounded, then a ferocious howl, and the kitchen seemed to explode with bodies.

Fur flew through the air as Charmer seemed to be everywhere at once. Barks and growls mixed with Gultcher's yell, then a howl that could have come from either one.

The hand around Opal's wrist loosened, and she pulled away, scrambling to her feet as the man and dog both went down.

Charmer had never attacked a soul since she'd known him, never even growled at a person, but he unleashed all his vicious fury on Gultcher now. Opal lunged for the door. This was her chance to get out of that man's way.

But once she reached the opening, she stalled, gripping the wood for support. She couldn't leave Charmer in there at Gultcher's whim. Although the dog seemed to have the upper hand at the moment. Blood ran down the man's wrist where he was trying to push away Charmer's bared teeth.

If she called the dog off, though, Gultcher would be as dangerous as an angry bear. She had to get help first.

Sprinting from the room, she aimed for the front door. Mr. and Mrs. Shumeister had walked to the mercantile since the weather was so fair. Maybe she could catch someone in the street who would help.

She jerked open the heavy wooden door, and almost plowed into Mr. S.

His brows formed a concerned V as he scanned her disheveled attire. "What's wrong? Who's that yelling?"

He pushed past her into the house as a loud yelp rang out, followed by a man's bellow.

"'Tis Gultcher." Opal charged after him, trying to catch her breath. "He tried to attack…"

Her words died in her throat as Mr. S. stopped at the desk in the corner of the dining room and withdrew a pistol from the top drawer. Did he plan to use it? That was what she'd wanted—someone to come in and take charge of the situation. But bloodshed in her kitchen?

Mr. S. held the handgun ready as he pushed open the kitchen door, peering around the edge.

"Halt." His sharp command seemed almost foreign, as though it didn't belong in this room. Of course, neither did the other shouts and snarls and barks.

All sound ceased at his order. Or maybe at sight of the gun.

With one hand pointing the pistol into the kitchen, Mr. S. pushed the door open wider. Gultcher half-sat, half-lay on the floor by the work counter, staring at Mr. S. with so much venom swirling in his dark eyes, Opal had to force herself not to duck out of sight.

How much was this man capable of? If they sent him away, would he try to retaliate? There was no jail in Mountain Bluff. No lawman of any kind. Just a town full of decent people who preferred a quiet life.

A movement to the side grabbed her attention. Charmer slunk into sight, almost crawling on his belly. Had he been hurt? "Here, boy. Come." She tapped her leg to call the dog, afraid to say anything else lest she distract Mr. S. from the control he had over that rapscallion. But she had to get the dog out of there. If Gultcher charged and Mr. S. were forced to shoot, she couldn't risk him getting caught in the fray.

"Gultcher, I'll give you one chance to explain yourself."

She'd never heard that biting undertone in Mr. S.'s voice. With the sun streaming through the window casting shadows on his face, he emanated the fierceness of an army general. A warrior seasoned by many years battle.

Gultcher must have seen it, too, because for the first time in their short-lived acquaintance, he seemed to shrink back. "I came asking for a bite to eat, and she started trying to entice me. I hadn't even touched her when this mongrel attacked. You'd best turn that gun on the cur a'fore he kills somebody." The man motioned a bloody arm toward Charmer, who'd taken up guard beside Mr. S.

"Opal." Without turning toward her, he spoke her name in that same tone of steel determination.

Panic ignited in her chest. Surely, he didn't believe the spoutings of this despoiler. He couldn't.

But, of course he did. Just like her father had, all those years ago when their steward first accosted Tori. Father wouldn't even consider that Jackson, his favored helper, might be lying. He immediately assumed the man would speak the truth, and Tori, only a girl, should be expected to invent stories. It was what weak-minded females did.

But she'd thought Mr. Shumeister was different. And maybe she still had a chance to make him believe her.

Raising herself to her full height, she gave her explanation. "He came in demanding coffee and the rolls Mr. Lefton had purchased. I told him those were spoken for and luncheon would be ready in a couple of hours." As she spoke the words, she saw the situation as he must see it. She dropped her gaze from his face. "I should have prepared food for him. I'm sorry." Had she truly brought this on herself? She knew how violent men like him could become when thwarted. If she'd been meek and provided a plate of food like she'd been hired to do, this whole debacle could have been avoided.

"Vat happened next?" Mr. Shumeister's tone remained solid, yet his accent seemed to grow thicker.

"He approached me, saying he thought I wanted his attentions. I told him he must be mistaken."

"And then vat?"

She swallowed down the mass clogging her throat. "Charmer attacked him."

"For no reason? Did this man touch you?"

Nodding, she did her best to hold back the burn in her eyes. "He came closer, and I threw bread dough at him. He grabbed my wrist, and that's when the dog charged." Would they make her leave? Surely, they would. They couldn't have this kind of disruption in their home. They couldn't have their employees denying service to patrons, nor dogs of employees viciously attacking those customers. But she'd always worked hard for them, and if he fired her, where would she go? Where would she find another job where she felt so safe? Maybe, if she begged, she could still salvage her work here.

She forced herself to keep her focus at least on his face, even though she couldn't quite meet his eyes. "I'm sorry, sir. It won't happen again, you have my word. Charmer will stay outside, away from the boarders. I promise." She'd have to tie him up, maybe in the shed. Although what a pitiful existence that would be. She could find someplace better for the dog who'd saved her, surely.

"Nein." He returned his full focus to Gultcher. "You will leave here. If you are injured, you can see the doctor first. Then you will leave and not come back to zis town. Do you understand?"

Gultcher's eyes narrowed. "You can't run me out."

"I can. If you come back to zis town again, you will be shot by anyone who sees you. No one will allow your face here. You have my word."

And between the force of his tone and the rigid command of his stance, 'twas hard to think his words could be anything but true.

Gultcher pushed to his feet, muttering something she was grateful she wasn't close enough to hear.

Mr. Shumeister eased back into the dining room to allow the man to pass, still aiming the gun at him. "Do you need ze doctor?"

"Nein." Gultcher spoke the word in a mocking accent. Then he spat on the floor as he stomped by them. He mumbled under his breath again, and Opal heard just enough to flare her defenses. The Shumeisters didn't deserve to be disparaged because of their uprightness. Nor because of their ancestry or the nation of their birth.

Yet Mr. S.'s expression never wavered as he followed several paces behind the man. "We go upstairs to get your zings."

As they tromped up the staircase, Opal scanned the room. After seeing to Charmer's injuries, she should set the kitchen to rights before Mr. Shumeister came back downstairs. Because then, surely, he would bid her gather her things and leave.

Chapter Seven

*O*pal checked over the exhausted dog. One small scratch seemed to be his only wound. The blood on his fur must have been Gultcher's.

Satisfied Charmer was all right, she turned her focus to the kitchen as the dog found a resting spot in the corner out of her way. After scrubbing the spots of blood on the floor, putting the biscuits in the oven, disposing of the bread dough she'd thrown at Gultcher, and putting to rights the supplies under the work counter that had been scattered in the fracas, she finally heard the front door open and close.

Her stomach had tied itself in so many knots, that morning's tea kept threatening to revisit her. But she forced herself to face the kitchen door with her back straight. In just a moment, it would open to seal her fate.

It did open, but 'twas Mrs. S. who charged in. "Liebling, what has happened?" She headed straight for Opal, switching to German as she wrapped her arms around her in a fierce hug.

Not at all the response Opal had prepared for, and it took several moments before her body could summon a response. Even a wooden one. "I'm sorry." She cupped Mrs. S.'s elbows, yet tried to keep a little distance between them, some separation for her emotions. If she gave in to the embrace, the tears burning her eyes might gain control. And she had to be strong, no matter how sad this parting would be.

Mr. S. had entered the room behind his wife, stopping a couple steps inside. As she raised her focus to him, he met her gaze with a sadness that pressed on her chest. But at least it gave her the strength to pull away from Mrs. Shumeister. She would ask for another chance, but if they refused, she'd leave quietly. The last thing she wanted was to make this harder on these good people.

Dropping her gaze to the floor at his feet, she gripped her hands together. She swallowed to summon some moisture into her parched mouth. "I'm sorry I caused so much trouble. I didn't—" She stopped herself just before an excuse slipped out. She had to take responsibility, prove she could do better.

Straightening her spine, she tried again. "I should have prepared food for him when he asked. I promise I won't let it happen again. I'll serve you and your guests well if you'll let me stay on. I give you my word."

Mrs. S. slipped a hand around her elbow—a strong hand—and turned Opal to face her. "You did nothing wrong." The words came out almost as a demand. Angry.

Opal couldn't stop herself from shrinking back, but Mrs. S. wasn't finished. "That man. That...*schurke*. He did wrong. You, liebling, did not. I am so sorry for what he did."

Her voice grew gentler with those last words, and she reached up to cup Opal's cheek. The tender affection in Mrs. S.'s expression—in her eyes and touch—pierced through the wall of strength she'd been trying to build.

Through the tears blurring her vision, she focused on the older woman. "Does that mean I can stay?"

"Ja, of course. We would not let you go with zat man roaming about, even if you wanted to."

It seemed too good to be possible. She tried to swallow down a sob and failed as part of it escaped anyway. But she had to know for sure. Turning to Mr. Shumeister, she searched his gaze for her verdict. He was the man of the house, no matter how much his wife seemed to run the place. And he'd certainly risen to the occasion when he'd pointed a gun at Gultcher.

Those faded blue eyes she'd come to love returned her gaze. Staring back at her with tenderness that even rivaled that of his wife. "You cannot leave us, *tochter*. This was not your fault. I am only sorry he was given the chance to frighten you." Then his gaze tracked down to Charmer, who still lay in the corner as though the episode had exhausted him. "I thank our Father in heaven that He sent this angel to protect you."

Apparently, Charmer understood the compliment, because he rose to his feet and padded over to tuck into her skirts. She stroked his head, taking the momentary distraction to gather her blooming emotions.

Charmer raised his doting brown eyes to gaze at her.

"I bet you've never been called an angel before, have you, boy?"

Matthias dismounted from Karl as he scanned the backyard of the Shumeister's boardinghouse. All looked the same as when he left four weeks ago, except for the six inches of fresh, powdery snow that had fallen the night before. Several sets of boot prints marred the white blanket in a trail from the back door to the outhouse, and it looked like some kind of animal track padded beside the human prints. One of the boarders must have brought a dog. What did Mutti think about that?

He settled Karl in his usual stall in the shed near the woods, then grabbed his saddle bags and the bundle of meat and furs he'd gathered and headed for the house.

Vatti wasn't in the sitting room where Matthias expected him, but voices and heavenly smells drifted from the kitchen. His feet followed the aromas, almost of their own accord.

Cracking the door, he poked his head into the room and paused to take in the activity. Mutti stood at the stove, stirring something in a flat pan, while Opal worked at the counter with her back to him. Her body moved in a lithe, steady rhythm with her efforts. More than a little

70

mesmerizing. Every part of her petite frame was perfectly proportioned, from the determined set of her shoulders to the tiny waist perfectly accented by her apron string and the drooping bow fastened in it.

"Sehr schön, ja?"

Mutti's words snapped him from his temporary paralysis, and he turned to see her watching him, a smirk pulling up one side of her mouth. It took him a moment to remember the translation with his very limited knowledge of the German language. *Very beautiful.* Ja. But he couldn't let himself be sidetracked by Opal's comeliness.

He straightened and stepped into the room, ignoring the sensations that sprung to life as Opal turned to face him.

"Matthias. You're back." So maybe it was impossible to ignore the smile that bloomed over her face as she spoke his name.

He nodded, then pulled the bundle from over his shoulder and turned to Mutti. "More venison here and some new furs. I can tan them if I'm around when the weather is warmer."

"How did your trip go?" Opal looked at him, an expectant smile on her face, as Mutti took the bundle and moved to the other side of the room. "Did you find anything out about your sister?"

He forced himself to return her gaze as he answered, but that required he brace himself against the power her attention seemed to have over him. Had it been like this the last time he was here? Maybe his awareness of her had something to do with the dreams he'd been having lately. Dreams where she came to him and he held her in his arms. Dreams where he was the strong protector, not a man whose impulsive actions tended to make things worse for those around him.

She was still waiting for his answer, and her expression changed from expectation to concern.

"I didn't find out much. Spoke to a lot of people, some who remembered them. Last anyone knew, my sister still lived with my aunt and uncle when they left town. No one had any idea where they'd gone, although some seemed to think north. No one could remember if that was just an assumption or based on something my uncle said."

It was hard to say all that without showing his disappointment. This was the first real lead he'd found...and lost.

"So what do you do next? We didn't expect to see you again so soon." Her gaze searched his face.

And he hadn't planned to come back so soon. Except that Mutti or Vatti might need him during the winter months. At least, that's the way he'd justified his intense desire to return to this place. He shrugged. "I sent queries to all the towns north of there for a couple hundred miles. I'll wait and see if any respond with information. The country's too big to try to cover it all on horseback."

She seemed to accept his answer. And what he'd said was true. Yet, it would have been easier to stay in Jackson to wait for the responses, and it possibly would have saved him extra travel if he received information from a town to the north.

But he couldn't seem to control his craving to come back here. So he'd ridden hard for a week, through the snow and freezing temperatures. And now he'd arrived. And standing here in this kitchen, taking in the sights and aromas around him, made it all seem worth it.

He'd come back.

Opal tried to focus on the dough for her strudel as Matthias answered Mrs. S.'s questions and asked his own about the happenings in Mountain Bluff. The Shumeisters hadn't expected him back for several months, which must account for the surge of joy that had exploded in her chest at the sight of him. The emotions were still fluttering in her midsection like a dancing troupe.

"Have you had any new boarders?" Matthias sat in the kitchen chair, sipping coffee.

Opal forced herself to keep working, trying not to stiffen as her mind skittered to an image of Mr. Gultcher. Even though the man had been gone for a week, the fear could still make her cower if she let it.

"Ja. A man who hunted for gold in ze mountains. He is gone now." Mrs. S. motioned from her position at the stove. "And Opal has a new special friend who stays around ze place."

She glanced sharply at Mrs. Shumeister. A special friend? The woman's face held no change from her normal, no-nonsense expression. But then she slid a glance to Opal. Stoic Mrs. Shumeister couldn't be…teasing. Could she?

"Who is he?" Something about Matthias's tone made her turn to him. His eyebrows had lowered, and he was looking straight at her, as though he expected her to account for the comment.

Something about the way he almost glared at her made a giggle spring up in her chest. She hadn't made the ridiculous statement, nor was it true in the sense that he assumed. She raised her chin. "He is a charming fellow. Always pleasant and most doting."

That seemed to set him back a notch, and she could almost see a struggle playing across his face. But a struggle for what? Did he think he might need to defend her honor? He certainly was chivalrous enough to jump to her protection at the first sign of trouble. So very different from Mr. Gultcher.

Different from any man she knew, really. Tori had been right when she'd said men of good character *did* exist. She hadn't found many in her life so far, but every part of her knew without a doubt Matthias was such a man.

Despite the fact he was now glaring at her.

"A *charming fellow*? Here in Mountain Bluff?" He turned his accusing stare back to Mrs. S. "What's his name?"

Opal bit her lip to hold in that giggle. And at that very moment, the kitchen door pushed open and Charmer padded into the room. His honey coat looked so much better now that she'd bathed and brushed him, and he no longer limped from his battle with Gultcher. He walked to her side and turned to face the others as he sat. Her perfect gentleman. "Look, here he is now. My little Charmer."

She braved a glance at Matthias, who stared at the dog with more than a little disbelief.

"You have a dog? In the kitchen?" He looked over at Mrs. S. "Who does it belong to?"

She motioned. "To Opal."

Matthias turned his gaze back to her, and this time a hint of a twinkle flickered in his eye. "So this is your charming fellow, eh?"

She nodded. "Most pleasant." Although she tried to keep her mouth from smiling, her cheeks probably gave her away.

Matthias watched her, and the solidness of his gaze was too much to look at, so she turned back to her work.

"Well, I'm headed to the telegraph office." His boots scuffed on the wooden floor as he rose from his chair, but she didn't turn to look. "I'll be back for dinner."

Although it shouldn't, the thought stirred a tingle of excitement in her chest.

Matthias gripped the papers in his fist as he stepped back into the boardinghouse. A letter and a telegram, but neither for him. It seemed Miss Opal Boyd was the fortunate one today.

He'd kept himself from reading the wire, but a glance at the return address on the letter showed Atlantic City, which meant 'twas likely from her cousin.

But no response from any of his inquiries about Alanna. He hung his coat on the peg by the door and ran a frustrated hand through his hair.

The kitchen door opened and Opal herself walked though carrying a stack of plates in one hand and three mugs in the other. She glanced at him but didn't stop as she laid out the dishes in their place settings on the table. "From that scowl, I assume you didn't receive any good news?"

Was he scowling? He schooled his features and stepped forward. "Nothing for me, but a letter and telegram for you."

She paused and turned to him with eagerness all over her expression. "Really?" She almost snatched the papers from his hand, and as she stared down at them, a crease formed across her brow. "I wonder why she would send a telegram."

Something about her tone, or maybe her hesitation, stirred a tenderness in his chest. He made his voice as gentle as he could. "You can open it and see."

She looked up at him, her gaze searching his eyes. Almost as though she were looking for answers there. Or maybe just reassurance. "I suppose I should."

Should he offer to read it to her? But before he could follow that thought, she snatched the missives from him.

He kept his focus on her face as she opened the telegram and read it, her gaze skimming back and forth along the text. And then her expression blanched. Her lips moved as though she were rereading the note under her breath, then she looked up at him, a wild desperation flashing in her eyes. "I have to go."

His chest seized as she spun away, moving toward the kitchen.

"What is it? What's wrong?" He followed her, the urgency in her movements striking a chord of fear in him.

"It's Tori." She pushed through the kitchen door, disappearing on the other side.

He slipped in behind her, but she was already spilling her news to Mutti, who sat at the table cutting shapes from dough.

"I have to go to her. Josiah's note didn't say whether she and the baby were safe, just to come when I could. May I leave now?" She was pinching the edges of the paper so hard it might tear any moment.

Mutti pushed to her feet. "Ja, of course. But not now, go tomorrow morning when you can start early. Matthias will go with you." She motioned at him with a solemn nod.

He would? How had he been commandeered into this excursion?

But then Opal turned to him with an expression so vulnerable, he had to swallow down a lump in his throat.

He nodded to her. "Of course. Tomorrow morning. We'll leave at first light."

Chapter Eight

"Here is ze food for you both. Make sure you get oats for ze horses from Herr Lefton. And here is a gift for ze child."

Opal accepted the wrapped bundle from Mrs. S. and tried to force a smile. They'd worked together on the tiny quilt in the evenings while Mr. S. read aloud from the Bible. "Please pray I use it to snuggle a healthy baby." She still didn't know whether Tori and the little one had survived the early delivery. Josiah's note had been so cryptic, and there wasn't time to send and receive a return telegram. The letter from Tori had been sent two days before the wire. So, for now, all she could do was worry and pray.

"Ja. I have spoken to ze Lord about it." Mrs. S. gripped her shoulders and pulled her into a motherly hug. "Remember the Scripture, 'Be anxious for nothing but in everything give zanks.'"

Opal soaked in the warm comfort of the verse and the embrace that snuggled her. 'Twas easier not to worry when Mrs. S. seemed so confident. As if the situation were completely under control. *Help me trust, Lord.* Her fledgling faith had so much to learn.

After a long moment, Mrs. S. pulled away with a sniff. "Go on. Matthias said he will meet you at the edge of town."

She nodded, sniffing back her own emotions. "Thank you. Are you sure you don't mind keeping Charmer?"

The older woman waved the question away. "Of course not. Go."

At the livery, Mr. Lefton was giving directions to the boy who cleaned stalls but stopped to greet her when she entered the barn. "You need a horse today?"

"Yes. Butter, please, if it isn't too much trouble."

"I'll have him ready in two minutes." The brawny man saluted, then turned on his heel and strode down the dim hallway.

He was always so helpful, and even the stable boy seemed to enjoy working for him. It made no sense why he would be at odds with Matthias.

Mr. Lefton was true to his word, leading the bay gelding she usually rode to the barn's entrance within only a few minutes of her request. "Butter here's had his breakfast and should be ready for some morning exercise. Will you be gone long?"

Opal took the reins and stroked the gelding's neck. "Yes, actually. I'm going to visit my cousin who's just delivered her first child. I received word late yesterday that I missed the birth, so I'm eager to see them both healthy."

Saying it that way might help soothe the dread that had been eating at her all night.

"Is that your cousin who lives several days ride from here? Will Shumeister be traveling with you, then?"

He remembered where Tori lived? But then, he'd met her when she came to find Ezra a little over a year before. That was when Ezra had first found the job for them with the Shumeisters, then he became deathly sick from a wound on his arm. "Yes, that's the cousin I'm visiting. Mr. Shumeister won't be accompanying me this time." Should she mention Matthias so the man didn't worry for her safety? 'Twas none of his affair, in truth, but she didn't want to leave him uneasy.

"I don't think it's safe for you to travel that distance alone, Miss Boyd." He glanced around, as if hoping to find someone to accompany her standing in the corner of his barn.

"Have no fear, Mr. Lefton. Matthias Björk will be riding with me. I'll be perfectly safe."

He spun back to face her, his expression morphing in the space of a second. His cheeks and neck mottled red as his brows sank into an angry V. "That killer? I wouldn't trust him with a skunk I hated. You'd be safer on a raging battlefield than with that two-faced renegade. I can't—"

"Mr. Lefton." She put every ounce of indignation she could muster into the words. Anything to stop his ranting. "Mr. and Mrs. Shumeister have asked him to accompany me. They obviously trust him with the task, and I've seen no reason to question that regard."

"Miss Boyd, I can't in good conscience allow you—"

"Thank you for your concern, Mr. Lefton, and for saddling Butter. Now, I must be off." With her chin high, she turned her back to the man, placed her foot in the stirrup, and mounted.

The burn of his frustration did its best to drive flaming arrows through her winter coat, but she stiffened her resolve. "Good day, Mr. Lefton."

With a nod, she reined her horse toward the street and Matthias. It was time to see Tori.

Matthias glanced at the woman riding beside him. They'd been on the trail for a good hour so far, and she'd not said more than a handful of words. But at least her face didn't look as stoic as it had when they'd started. Her mouth wasn't forming that pinched line that stole the fullness from her lips. The set of her shoulders had softened, too, letting her move with the horse in an easy rhythm. Not unlike the time they'd ridden to see the geyser.

Yet this time seemed different. Maybe it was his imagination, but he didn't remember being so painfully aware of her presence every moment. Each time she reached up to brush a wisp of hair from her cheek, or when she leaned forward to stroke her mare's neck, he had to force himself not to stare at her. Every movement so graceful and poised. Like a woodland nymph.

If only she didn't seem so locked in her own thoughts.

"You said your cousin lives near her husband's kin?" Maybe a question would get her talking.

"Yes. Mara and her family live across the river."

"Must be nice to have relations so close." He could only imagine how good that would feel. One day he might have the same. If he ever found Alanna.

She nodded but didn't speak again, so he let the silence settle for a few minutes. They had a long trip ahead—two days of riding together. Surely she'd soften as the journey progressed.

But she didn't speak again for almost an hour. And it seemed like a wall was growing up between them, an invisible barrier. Why did that bother him so? He didn't want to get close to another person, especially Opal. The people around him always ended up hurt from one of his rash decisions, so he'd learned long ago to keep a distance.

Yet even as his mind told his body to still his tongue, his mouth opened of its own accord. "So how do you like Mountain Bluff? Does it suit your tastes?" The little hamlet was quieter than any other town he'd seen—and he'd traveled to every settlement, village, and city in the Wyoming Territory and beyond—in his search for Alanna.

"I like it very much." Was that a touch of feeling in her tone? Her face had softened into a gentle smile as she flicked a quick glance at him.

"'Tis not too quiet? I'd imagine a lady like you is accustomed to a fine city with dressmakers and milliners at your disposal."

Her pretty brows lowered into a V, and that smile disappeared from her face. Which made him wish he could bite the words back, although they shouldn't have made her sad.

"Boiling Springs wasn't a large city, and I don't miss the other. I'd much rather have a quiet town like Mountain Bluff. I love my work with the Shumeisters."

He nodded. "I know they're grateful to have you. Vatti talks about you as if you're his own daughter, and Mutti relies on you. I'm glad you're there to help. Things were getting to be too much for them before. And they obviously love you."

She turned to him with so much hunger in her blue gaze, it made his gut clench. "You think so?"

He swallowed to push down the way his body reacted to her. "Of course." Who couldn't love her? And not just because she quietly accomplished ten times more than most women every day. From the loyalty and affection she gave the Shumeisters to the gentle way she'd rescued that yellow dog. And if he'd had any doubt about her noble character, the way the animal seemed enamored of her was enough to convince him. Animals could sense a villain, but Miss Opal Boyd had clearly won over that dog she called Charmer—both heart and belly.

"And what of you?" Her question pulled him from his thoughts. "You said you grew up in this territory. Your upbringing must have been thrilling."

A parade of youthful antics slipped through his mind. The time he'd climbed one of the steeper peaks at the edge of the Crackens' grazing pasture. He'd lost his footing and tumbled backward down the rocky incline but walked away with only scrapes and a broken arm.

Another summer when he'd gone to retrieve the milk cow from a pasture, he'd noticed a set of mountain goat tracks and followed them into the rocky area. Unfortunately, he'd been so engrossed in his tracking, he hadn't seen the rattlesnake sunning itself until just before it struck. At least he'd been wearing a pair of oversize boots, and the leather had soaked up most of the snake's venom.

Still, his foot had swollen and the skin had turned black for days. Just one more injury Mrs. Cracken had needed to nurse him through. It was a wonder the family didn't turn him out long before he left on his fourteenth birthday.

"Too thrilling for words?"

He blinked, forcing himself back to the present. He turned a glance to her as her words registered.

She was looking at him with a kind of half smile, her head cocked as though she were trying to decipher his thoughts.

"No, not too thrilling. I mean…'twas thrilling, but I did a lot of boyish antics that made things harder on the family who raised me." He swallowed down the pain that always clogged his throat when he remembered the longsuffering sighs he'd elicited from Mrs. Cracken.

"You were young, weren't you? I would expect at least a few boyish antics." Opal's soft tone only made him want to cringe.

85

"I'm afraid I gave my guardians more trouble than they bargained for when they took me in." But really, why was he telling her all this? The past was best stuffed away.

"What happened to your parents?"

"They died." He didn't want to be rude, but he didn't usually share such details.

Thankfully, she didn't press the point like a lot of females might have.

He eased out a long breath and settled into the silence he should have been thankful for from the beginning.

Opal huddled under her blankets that night, trying to keep every scrap of heat from escaping the covers. She'd insisted on pushing as far as they could, which meant darkness had settled by the time they'd stopped for the night. The easiest spot they'd found to camp still had patches of snow littering the ground. And if the freezing temperatures and laden sky meant anything, they might have a fresh layer of the icy stuff by morning.

Matthias had wanted to build a shelter for her to sleep under, but she'd insisted it wasn't necessary. That she'd slept under the stars before and could handle it without concern. She didn't include the fact that those nights had been only the two other times she'd traveled to and from Mountain Bluff, and the weather on those trips had never been this bone-chilling cold.

She glanced at Matthias, who lay on the other side of the fire, tucked under what looked like a well-used buffalo or bear hide. The firelight danced on the side of his tanned face, turning the scruff on his cheek golden. His features were so strong, with solid angles that made him seem more than capable.

Was he asleep? His chest rose and fell in a slight rhythm, but he wasn't snoring or even breathing hard through parted lips. Somehow, 'twas hard to imagine him snoring, but…he was a man, wasn't he?

Suddenly, his eyelid raised, and he turned to glance at her. Had he felt her staring at him? She wanted to look away, but he'd already caught her.

The corner of his mouth curved. "Can't sleep?"

She snuggled deeper under the quilt. "'Tis colder than I thought it would be."

His brows lowered in a frown as his gaze scanned the length of her blanket. Then he sat up and pushed to his feet. "We can make this fire bigger." He tossed several logs onto the flames from the stack he'd gathered earlier.

The campfire sparked and blazed with the added fuel, and she strained to feel the heat of it as he moved back to lean over his sleeping pallet.

He straightened and turned to her, and before she realized what he intended, he stepped to her and spread the top fur from his bedroll over her blankets. "This should help keep the warmth in. There's nothing much better than a grizzly skin."

"But…no. I can't take yours." Yet the heaviness of the covering gave an instant infusion of warmth that she clung to.

He turned away. "I've still got a stack of furs. Sorry I didn't think about it earlier." He settled back on his blankets and leaned against the tree behind him instead of lying down. With one hand propped on his knee, he stared into the fire.

She sank into the warmth of her covering, letting her muscles relax as the heat enveloped her. She should insist Matthias take the pelt back, but she couldn't quite bring herself to. Maybe he wouldn't be able to sleep now because of the chill.

He sat there with a thoughtful expression on his face, almost brooding. Although that may be the way the firelight flickered over some areas of his face and cast others into shadow.

Something about the sight of him there started a longing in her chest. What forces in his life had shaped him into the man he was today? What did he want from life? To live on his own in the mountains for the rest of his days? To hunt and wander and fade in and out of people's lives?

Before she lost her nerve, she spoke. "If you could accomplish anything you wanted, what would it be?"

His gaze rose from the fire to her face and locked there a long moment. She met his look, trying to keep her expression soft so she didn't scare him off with such a deep question. Would he answer it or shrug her off?

At last, he turned to stare into the darkness outside the firelight. "I would find my sister."

Ah, yes. She should have guessed that would be his deepest wish. "I'm sure if I had a sister whom I'd been separated from, I would do anything I could to find her. That's the way I feel about Tori. She's my cousin, but really more like a sister."

He looked back at her, a softness in his eyes. "I'm sure she'll be glad to see you."

That angst from earlier bubbled in her chest again. "I hope I'm not too late."

"Have you prayed about it?"

The question caught her off guard, yet he said it as though prayer were a common topic of conversation between them. She struggled to return his solid stare. "Yes. A lot." Almost every moment of their ride, she'd been raising a litany to heaven.

He nodded. "Then you've done all you can. The rest is in God's hands."

The conviction of his words washed through her like a wave, stinging her eyes and balling a knot of emotion in her throat so she couldn't speak. Instead, she nodded and focused on steady breathing to still her emotions.

"What about you? What would you choose if you could accomplish anything?"

She should have known that was coming and been prepared with an answer. What did she want most in life? Honestly, she'd already found it. A safe place. A quiet life where she could work at something she enjoyed. A hideaway where she didn't have to worry about advances from voracious men. Or at least, didn't have to worry about them going unpunished. Should she say any of that to Matthias?

"There must be something."

She nibbled her lower lip. "I guess I've already found what I wanted. A nice quiet life where I can help people. Somewhere safe."

Safe. That was a normal enough desire, wasn't it? Had she opened herself up too much? She stared into the flames, dreading what his response might be.

He was quiet for a long moment, then his baritone drifted across the circle. "And you think you've found it?"

She looked up at him. "I think so. It feels like I'm helping the Shumeisters. Do you not agree?" Why did she care what he thought anyway?

He bobbed his chin once. "Of course. They depend on you a great deal. I only meant the part about being safe. Mountain Bluff is a quiet town, but is any place ever really safe?"

A shiver ran down her spine, dispelling some of the warmth that shrouded her. Had the Shumeisters told him about Gultcher's advance? She forced the feeling down and leveled a glare at him. "Mr. Björk, compared to the life I once lived, Mountain Bluff is just shy of heaven."

Without another word, she turned away from the fire—away from him—and pressed her eyes shut. Why did he care about her life in Mountain Bluff, anyway?

Chapter Nine

The warmth surrounding her was too cozy to leave.

Opal opened her eyes to darkness and snuggled deeper under the covers. Yet, a glimmer of bright light showed around the edges of her vision. Had she pulled the blanket over her head?

She reached up to feel the dark form over her — the bear skin Matthias had let her use. As she eased it down, a blast of cold air assaulted her face. She squinted against the brightness of the morning light as it glared off a world of white snow. A drop of icy wet plopped onto her forehead, sending a shiver down her body.

She tucked the top of the blanket under her chin, trying to hold in the cocoon of warmth as she took in the surroundings. She must have slept through a good four or five inches of snowfall.

A glance at where Matthias had slept showed a rectangular patch of bare ground. Not only had he risen, but he'd already packed his bedroll. Or maybe hung it out to dry. Of course, it would only turn to icicles in this frigid air.

But if Matthias was already up and moving, she should be, too. Summoning her self-discipline, she pushed the pelt to the side—along with the layer of snow covering it—and rose to her feet. She pulled her coat tighter around her. She'd slept in full attire because of the cold, including fur hood and boots, and so at least she still had some protection.

A trail of boot prints led toward where they'd tied the horses, so she headed the opposite direction for a bit of privacy. Matthias would likely be hungry when he came back from tending the animals, so she should prepare some bread and cheese from the food bundle Mrs. S. had packed.

Within a few minutes, she had a meager breakfast laid out. 'Twas not the grand table of plenty Mrs. S. liked to prepare, but it would be enough to carry them through the morning's ride.

Matthias still hadn't returned, and she scanned the wintry scene through the trees in all directions. Maybe she should see if he needed help.

But the sound of boots crunching in the snow grabbed her attention, and Matthias became visible through the snow-laden branches. He looked so strong and rugged in his fur coat and cap—the epitome of a mountain frontiersman.

Something dangled from his right hand, and it wasn't until he drew closer that the details of the fur and limp body became clearer. He must have been hunting.

He stopped just outside of their campsite and crouched beside a tree. "If you'll start a fire, we can roast this meat."

"I laid out a cold breakfast for us. I didn't know you'd gone hunting."

He grunted. "Wasn't much of a hunt. Saw tracks in the snow and thought it'd be good to start with something warm. Won't take long to roast the meat on sticks."

Using the wood he'd covered before the snow fell, she kindled a fire in the bare spot where his blankets had been. Matthias had the meat prepared and separated into two portions—both speared through with sticks—before she had the fire built up enough to cook. He'd obviously done this more than once.

And he was right about it being worth the effort to cook something warm to fill their bellies on this cold morning.

In short order, they'd finished eating, packed up the camp, and mounted their horses.

Matthias glanced at her with raised eyebrows. "You ready?"

She nodded. "Ready." More than ready to see Tori and her baby. Hopefully by late afternoon she'd be cradling the tiny child in her arms.

A light snowfall drifted over the dusky landscape as they finally rode into the yard of the Rocky Ridge Stage Station that evening. A haze of familiarity filtered through Opal, like seeing an old friend. The place looked so peaceful, with only a few prints marring the snowy ground. Several horses munched hay in the corral behind the barn.

No people in sight, though. Had they moved to Mara and Josiah's farm to get help from family? She'd not been there when Tori needed her, so maybe her cousin had sought assistance with the baby elsewhere. She should be thankful that Ezra's family lived so near, that Tori had someone to lean on in a time of need.

But how badly was her need? Had the baby been born with an illness or defect from coming too soon? The muscles in her shoulders pulled as tight as the knot in her gut.

Matthias reined in at the front door of the cabin. "Let me have your horse, and I'll get them settled while you go in."

She jumped to the ground, but something held her back from charging to the door. Looking up at him, her teeth found her lower lip. "Do you think they're here?"

He nodded toward the cabin's roof. "There's smoke coming from the chimney."

She followed his gaze, then let out a long breath. "Good." Tori was in there, waiting for her.

Matthias waited on his big, gray gelding as she knocked at the door. It took only a moment before the shuffle of the latch sounded and the door pulled open to reveal a man.

Ezra. He blinked once, as though he couldn't quite believe the image on his doorstep, then jerked the door open wide. "Opal. You came."

94

He practically pulled her inside, then slipped an arm around her shoulder in a brotherly half-hug. "Tori will be so glad to see you." Then he seemed to catch sight of Matthias and stilled. "Howdy, I'm Ezra Reid."

She turned to make introductions, but Matthias was already nodding a greeting. "Matthias Björk. Mind if I settle the horses in your barn?"

"Of course. I'll come help." Ezra glanced at her. "Tori's in the bedroom. Go on in." The way his eyes crinkled at the corners in a fond smile started a longing in her chest. If she'd had a brother, she would want him to be just like Ezra. Although, in truth, now that he'd married Tori, he was just like a brother.

When the door closed behind Ezra, a silence settled over the large front room of the house.

She crept toward the back wall where two doors led to bed chambers. The one on the left should be her cousin's. "Tori?"

"Opal?" The voice came faintly through the closed door, but Opal couldn't deny the surge of excitement in her chest at the sound of Tori's call.

She opened the door slowly. "May I come in?"

"Of course. Come here." Tori's tone held that edge of impatience that marked her personality. She tended to charge ahead when she wanted something.

Opal opened the door fully and took in the sight of Tori, sitting up in the bed with a bundle of quilt in her arms. Her face nearly glowed as the smile enveloped her.

95

"Come here." Tori motioned for her, and Opal slipped forward to her cousin's side.

Her thought had been to hug Tori, but as she caught sight of a tiny hand in the cloth bundle, she stilled. "Oh…"

The tiniest face looked up at her, swaddled in a blanket cocoon. Those lips formed a perfect cupid's bow, yet they weren't any bigger than Opal's thumbnail. And that nose. Those eyes, as cornflower blue as her own. The sting of emotion rose up her throat, as she took in every perfect feature.

A hand moved in the bundle of cloth, tiny fingers splayed as the baby seemed to be waving at her.

"Hello, there, little angel." She stroked her finger over the baby's palm, and the little cherub moved her lips, almost like a baby bird receiving food from its mother. "You're precious."

"She is, isn't she?"

Opal looked up at her cousin, who was smiling at her babe as though the child were her heart and soul.

"She's beautiful, Tori. And are you both well?" Tori's face seemed to glow from joy, yet beneath, shadows smudged the skin under her eyes and faint lines marked their corners.

Tori met her gaze. "I'm tired, but…we're well." Her gaze dropped to her sweet one and all signs of weariness seemed to slip away.

Opal sank down to sit on the side of the bed and peered at the babe again. "What have you named her?"

"Ruby Anne."

Opal looked up at her as warmth flowed through her chest. "You gave her the same second name as me."

Tori gave her a soft smile and a nod. "And Ruby is a gemstone, too, like Opal. We want her to be as special as her aunt, yet her own person, too."

Now, not only could she not speak, but emotions climbing up her throat filled her eyes and threatened to spill over.

"Would you like to hold her?"

Little Ruby's eyes had drifted shut, her perfect lips still making that sucking motion.

"But she's sleeping." And she was so tiny. How fragile she must be. "Is she healthy?"

"Yes, thanks to our Lord. Even though she was almost a month early, she's eating well and already getting pudgy. See her little hands." Tori cradled one of the tiny arms to display dimples at Ruby's fingers and elbow.

The baby's eyes opened to half-mast, and she made a mewing sound as she shifted her head.

Tori extended the bundle of blanket and babe. "Here. She wants to meet her Aunt Opal."

She could barely breathe as she took the infant. So light, even swaddled in thick layers. Those blue eyes stared up at her, innocent and trusting. "Hello, my little Ruby. I'm so glad to finally meet you."

Ruby worked her lips like a baby bird again. So sweet, the ache in Opal's chest twisted tight enough to constrict her breathing. She would probably never have a babe of her own.

She'd never longed for the love of a man, not with all the wickedness she'd seen from that gender. But this innocent new life. How could she not want a child like this to nurture and love?

A noise sounded in the other room, helping her push back the tears that had already started to seep through her lashes. Then the low vibrato of male voices. She sniffed, and the baby squirmed in her arms. "You hear your papa?"

Ezra's face appeared in the doorway. "There's stew in the pot, Opal. We were just going to sit down to dinner."

Opal glanced back at Tori. "Oh, yes. Let me take over in the kitchen." She'd come here to help, after all. "Shall I bring you a tray?"

"No." Tori yawned and stretched an arm over her head. "Ezra's been babying me so, but I need to get back to my duties."

"Your most important job is a to be a mother." Ezra stepped near and planted a kiss on the top of Tori's head, then he leaned toward Opal and peered at his babe, who seemed to be staring up at him. "And you, sweet one, have been keeping your mama busy at all hours of the night, eh?"

The tenderness on his face tightened her chest even more. Tori had found a good man and such happiness here.

Ezra straightened. "Bring our girl out when you're ready, Opal. From the looks of things, she's found a set of arms she likes." He turned and left the room.

Opal eased to her feet, doing her best not to jostle the baby, whose eyes were drifting shut now that the excitement of seeing her papa had passed. "Do you need help getting ready?"

"No, I'm fine. Go out and show the baby to Mr. Shumeister. I'll be there in a moment."

Mr. Shumeister? She stared at her cousin for a moment before Tori's meaning came clear. "Oh, no. Mr. S. didn't come with me." But if she said who'd accompanied her, she knew exactly what expression would come over her cousin's face.

Tori eyed her with wary confusion. "You didn't travel all this way by yourself? Opal Anne Boyd. Don't you remember what happened to me when I attempted that? Why, 'tis a wonder—"

"I didn't. Stop your fretting."

Tori paused, staring at her with that look that meant her mind was spinning. "So who came with you?"

The heat crawled up her neck before she could stop it. But why was she embarrassed? Not because there was any special affection between her and Matthias. No, the burn that surely marked her face was because of what Tori would assume. That was all.

Still, she ducked her head low as she cooed and murmured to the baby.

"The mountain man accompanied you all the way from Mountain Bluff?" The incredulous tone in Tori's voice only made it worse. "You were alone with him two days and a night? Oh, Opal. You have to tell me everything."

Tori jumped to her feet, not giving a second for Opal to speak if she'd wanted to. "No, you'll tell me everything later. For now, I want to meet this man."

"I should go help Ezra." Opal moved around her cousin, heading for the door and the escape of that wooden barrier.

The men paused to look at her as she entered the main room. Her eyes instantly found Matthias, who stood at the table with a coffee pot, filling cups.

His gaze met hers, and the corner of his mouth tipped up. Then he looked at the bundle in her arms, and his expression softened. He looked like he might walk to her, but then he caught himself. Did he want to see the babe? She wouldn't have expected such a rugged man like him to care about a little infant. Yet, who couldn't love this sweet new life?

She approached him. "See our Ruby?" As she rounded the table, he leaned toward her, peering at the little cherub face tucked in the blankets. Opal fixed the covers so he could see Ruby's features better. "Isn't she perfect?"

He sucked in an audible breath. "She is. And so...tiny."

She couldn't help but smile at the way the child seemed to affect him.

He raised a hand as though he wanted to touch, but it stalled halfway up.

"Do you want to hold her?" She glanced at Ezra to make sure he didn't object. He nodded, although his gaze shifted to Matthias as though taking the man's measure.

"I...no...I..." Matthias stuttered and straightened to pull back a few inches. "I don't think so."

The way this little bundle of love made him so nervous and tongue-tied brought a giggle in Opal's throat. She pushed it down, but the merry sound escaped when she said, "Perhaps after we eat you can sit in a chair and rock her."

His wide eyes tracked up to her face, then back to the bundle. He didn't speak, but the way his throat bobbed resurrected her chuckle.

Chapter Ten

The simple meal of stew and biscuits was heavenly as it soaked through Opal to warm her core. Tori plied them with questions about their journey and the happenings at Mountain Bluff, but at least she didn't ask Matthias any pointed questions to embarrass her. At least, nothing as overt as inquiring about the man's intentions toward her. But the way Tori kept giving her raised eyebrow glances made it clear she'd have to face the inquisition later.

"So, will you be staying as long as Opal does, Matthias?" Ezra cradled his mug in both hands as he leaned back in his chair at the end of the meal. "We have a decent bunkhouse with beds and a cook stove. You're welcome to it as long as you'd like. Occasionally a stage passenger stays there, but we don't often have any who stay overnight." His gaze found his wife as the corners of his mouth tweaked.

Was he remembering when she and Tori had arrived on the stage and disembarked to stay for good? He'd had to scramble to find decent accommodations for them at his sister's ranch, but he'd never made them sleep in the bunkhouse.

Matthias leaned back in his chair, mirroring Ezra's at the other end of the table. "I appreciate the offer, but I've business south of here. I'll be heading out in the morning." He looked to Opal. "I'll be back when you're ready to return to Mountain Bluff. Just tell me when you think that will be." His voice softened as he spoke to her, and her traitorous heart did a flip.

She met his gaze, and her chest tightened at the concern shimmering there. If she let herself, it would be too easy to fall into this man's protection. His strength and care.

But she couldn't let herself. It would be foolish to rely on a man. Foolish to let her heart engage in their friendship. He was Mr. and Mrs. Shumeister's friend. She had to keep that distance.

She raised her chin a notch. "I don't know how long I'll stay, but I can return to the Shumeisters on my own when I'm ready. You needn't worry about accompanying me back."

To his credit, he didn't flinch or acknowledge the rebuff she'd just given him. Maybe 'twas only a set-back in her own mind. All the better. She didn't want to hurt him, only protect herself from getting too close.

"Are you happy, Opal?"

They'd barely settled after dinner, the men out feeding the stock for the night. Opal kept her focus on the babe snuggled in her arms as she relaxed into the steady rhythm of the rocking chair. Tori's question hung in the air, though. And she knew better to think Tori meant here and now, holding this sweet infant. Her cousin had always been a mother hen, despite the fact she was a few months younger.

At last, she looked up and smiled. "I am. The Shumeisters are good people, and I like my place there. They really need me." And how wonderful to be needed.

Tori studied her for another long moment, then she smiled. "I'm glad."

Little Ruby yawned, her mouth opening in a perfect O. Opal couldn't help but stroke her cheek. So soft.

She glanced up at Tori. "I don't have to ask if you're happy. I only need to see the way your face glows."

Tori's contented smile was almost too hard to look at, so Opal focused her attention on the cherubic face in her arms. "And what of you, sweet one? Are you happy?"

Ruby worked her mouth and made a soft mewling sound. Always pleasant, this child. Opal raised her brows at Tori. "Does she ever cry?"

Tori returned the look, but then a yawn engulfed her. "Especially at night when we should all be sleeping."

They slipped into easy silence as Opal studied the precious new life God had brought into their family. 'Twas easy to believe and praise a God who created such innocence.

"And what of your mountain man. Is he part of your happiness?"

She wanted to scowl at Tori, but even in the dim light of the fire beside them, the blush heating her cheeks probably showed. So she kept her head bent to watch the babe. "He's not my mountain man. And besides, I would think you'd warn me away from men instead of pushing me toward him." This time she did summon a glare for her cousin.

Tori's smile dimmed. "Part of me wants to protect you from him. Yet, I want you to have the same joy I've found with Ezra. It's not just any man who could bring you that joy, though. He must be the right one. A man who seeks to honor God by honoring you. Something inside makes me think Mr. Björk is that kind of man." She leaned forward in her chair. "What do you think, Opal? I've only just met him, so what does *your* heart tell you?"

Her heart? She was afraid to ask it. Instead, she shook her head. "My heart says nothing at all. It says I'm happy at the Shumeisters and all is well." She glanced up at Tori with a smile. "My heart says I've never been so content as I am right now, holding my little niece."

Tori leaned back in her chair with a sigh. The kind that said she'd let the subject drop. For now.

Matthias stared down into Opal's clear blue gaze. It would be so easy to be captured in their trance. Which meant 'twas time for him to leave.

"You said you have business south of here?" She swayed as she held the tiny bundle of baby up to her shoulder. Motherhood fit so perfectly on her. She should find a husband and raise a passel of babies. But that husband shouldn't be him. He'd be no good for her.

He turned away from the sight they made—woman and child. "In Superior. I need to check on responses to some queries I made about Alanna. Should be back in about two weeks. Will that be long enough for you?"

That would give him sufficient time to get her back to Mountain Bluff and fit in another hunting trip before the start of Yule. Mutti and Vatti would be counting on him to return in time, but if Opal wanted to stay longer, maybe he could work out a different arrangement. Do his hunting before he returned for her, or some such.

"Two weeks should be fine." Her voice was soft and drew his back to her. The tinge of sadness in her eyes stabbed like a knife in his chest.

"I can wait longer if you prefer."

She shook her head. "I need to get back to help the Shumeisters."

The sight of her there, looking so vulnerable, yet so determined... That was exactly why he needed to leave this place.

A bit of distance would help him remember why he was no good for her.

The sound of bells in the yard echoed through the stillness of the cabin as Opal kneaded bread dough later that afternoon. It seemed they had visitors, just when Tori and the baby finally collapsed into much-needed sleep. Ezra had gone to the barn to catch up on chores, so she'd taken the opportunity for some baking, which made it seem almost as if she'd never left Mountain Bluff.

After wiping her hands on a cloth, she turned toward the door. Ezra would greet their guests, but he might need help if it were another stage. The eastbound stage had already come that morning, but he said the westbound would come mid-afternoon if it didn't meet with trouble.

She grabbed her coat from the hook and pulled open the door. A sleigh sat in the yard, and it took a moment for her to recognize the people milling around it.

"Miss Opal!"

Katie's voice pulled her attention, honing her focus on the little bundled figure who was not nearly so little as she'd been only a few months ago. Had she grown a half foot in such short time?

Opal moved toward the group, and Katie met her midway with a fierce embrace. "My stars, how you've grown." Those arms around her waist had never felt so good.

Was there anything better than the love of a child? Although this girl was more young lady than child.

"Opal, you finally made it." Mara reached them, a thick bundle of cloth in one arm, she pulled Opal into a hug with her other. "We were worried about you traveling in this weather. I'm so glad you're safe."

Opal pressed her eyes shut to hold in the threatening tears. These people had become family in such a short time, taking in Tori and Opal like long-lost family. "I've missed you all." The words were barely more than a strangled whisper, but 'twas hard enough to push them past the lump in her throat.

Mara seemed to understand, for she held the embrace tightly for another moment, then eased back. "Well, you're home now, so we must celebrate." Her eyes glimmered as she studied Opal's face. "I'm so happy you're here."

Opal tried to offer a smile, but it felt a bit wobbly. She motioned toward the bundle. "Is this your little one? I'll bet he's grown so."

Mara nodded, a joyous smile pulling at her rosy cheeks. "The wagon always rocks him to sleep." She took Opal's hand and turned them toward the house. "Let's get out of this cold, and we'll see if we can't coax him awake."

Inside. She planted her feet as awareness sank through her. "Tori and the baby just fell asleep. I hate to wake them."

Mara nodded. "We'll use our whispering voices then. Katie, run help Papa and Uncle Ezra remember how to use their special voices, please."

"Yes, ma'am." Katie hesitated as she glanced at Opal. "But don't tell the interesting parts until I get there."

They made their way inside, and Mara worked to unbundle herself and the babe as Opal headed toward the kitchen. After putting on a fresh pot of coffee to simmer, she reached for the remaining biscuits and the wedge of cheese from dinner the night before. "I have a pot of beans cooking, but this will hold us over until they're ready."

"You can't have been here even a full day, Opal, and already you have this place in perfect order. I'm ever in awe of how you can be so competent without seeming to try."

Opal ducked away from the compliment as she placed a stack of plates on the table, though her face surely showed her embarrassment. "I'm not competent, I assure you. No matter how hard I try." She turned to Mara with a smile for the tousle-haired baby in her arms. "Now, let me see this young man. My, but he's even more handsome than before."

The next hours passed in pleasant succession as Mara and Katie peppered her with questions and she reveled in the baby exuberance of little Christopher. Josiah watched them all with an amused quirk to his mouth and the occasional lift of his brows. He was apparently used to being the quiet one in the group. From his chair near the fire, Ezra looked like he might be struggling to stay awake. Poor fellow. She should probably send him to nap with Tori.

It wasn't long before Tori emerged from the bedroom holding little Ruby as Opal was sitting on the floor with Mara's son. "Look. He's sitting almost by himself." She barely touched the tot at his lower back, more for balance than support.

"He'll be walking by Epiphany."

A choked gasp came from Mara, but Opal ignored it. Instead she shot Tori a sly glance. "The holiday is what, three weeks away? I think you're right. He'll be walking and eating Christmas goose."

The days passed in a whirl of visiting and housekeeping and sweet baby snuggles, not to mention buckets of dirty nappies and more laundry than she'd thought possible. Thankfully, Ezra handled the twice-daily stages with little disruption to the family. She did her best to keep a steady supply of food for the weary travelers and found herself relying more and more on the endless stewpot Mrs. S. had taught her to keep simmering.

'Twas nearing the end of the fortnight—two weeks on the morrow, actually—which meant Matthias would return for her soon. Her treasured days with Tori and the family were almost at an end.

Yet the thought of his arrival didn't have the sour taste she would have expected since it signaled the end of her time here. In fact, part of her craved it. Did she miss the Shumeisters so much? She prayed for them each morning as she read her daily Scripture, and the images her mind recalled of their dear faces always brought a smile. Surely, they wouldn't deny her this time with her cousin and her new precious babe. And she didn't feel guilty about being away.

She just…longed for something. And Matthias's coming must be a placeholder, a direction for her longing to take hold.

But just now, as she stirred cornmeal batter for johnnycakes with little Ruby tucked in a sling around her neck, she could imagine herself being content to do this every day for the rest of her life. Mostly.

The crunch of boots in the snow sounded outside the door. Ezra must have returned from picking up fresh stage horses at Josiah and Mara's ranch.

But then a knock sounded on the door, sending a tingle of dread to raise the fine hairs on her neck. Ezra wouldn't knock. Tori was taking a much-needed nap in the bed chamber. Should she wake her?

Ezra said there wouldn't be any more stages today, and besides, the stage drivers always called from the yard to make their presence known. As if the thundering hooves of the horses weren't notice enough. The nearest neighbor—other than Josiah and Mara—was several hours away, and 'twas not likely someone would ride that distance to come calling in six inches of icy snow.

She crept toward the door, her eyes scanning the wall above the fireplace, then around the room. There. Above the door hung a rifle.

Reaching up to the tips of her toes, she gripped the cool wood and pushed up to remove it from the hooks. Would she even be able to shoot the thing? Tori had insisted they both learn before Opal moved to Mountain Bluff, and Ezra had spent several patient hours helping them practice. But that had been over a year ago.

No matter. Hopefully this visitor wouldn't be a threat. Or if danger appeared on the doorstep, maybe one glimpse down the barrel of this gun would send the person skittering.

She wrapped a hand protectively around the sleeping baby, then inhaled a breath and made her voice sound as gruff as possible. "Who's there?"

"Matthias Björk."

The wave of relief that seeped through her nearly washed the strength out of her legs. She leaned the rifle against the wall, then gripped the door latch and pulled, leaning hard on it for support.

"Opal?" The familiar hood appeared first, then Matthias's rugged face. Those green eyes. Across his jaw and cheeks, several days' worth of golden scruff covered his tanned skin.

The sight of him did something strange in her chest, making her legs feel like they would melt any second. She moved her other hand to hold onto the door, too.

"What's wrong?" He was there in an instant, gripping her elbow. His arm went around her back, supporting her.

A good question. Clenching her jaw, she straightened, the weight of the baby in the sling heavy at her neck. "I'm fine, just…" She stepped back, putting space between them. "I lost my balance, is all."

He seemed to gather himself as well, but studied her. His gaze dropped to the bundle around her neck, and his expression softened. "The babe is well?"

Opal glanced down and slipped a hand under Ruby to support her. "Very well." She hadn't stirred once in the past half hour. "If we could only get her to sleep this heavily at night, her mother would be just as well."

He leaned forward, and she pulled down the side of the sling so he could get a better look.

In just these last two weeks, Ruby had filled out so much. Her little cheeks were rounding nicely, and she still had those perfect lips.

"She trusts you." Matthias was close enough that this breath brushed her face.

The feel of it stole her thoughts, and she inhaled quickly to make her mind work. "I think the way the sling rocks while I work puts her to sleep so soundly. And she likes to be bundled inside it."

She had to force herself to think of what to do next. "You must be cold and hungry. I have stew ready, and coffee. Come and sit."

His gaze drifted to meet hers, holding her there. She should fill a trencher for him, but the strength of his focus seemed to draw her. The lines around his eyes showed just how tired he was, yet his charisma hadn't dwindled one bit.

For a moment, some insane part of her wanted to step into his arms. To feel the strength of him surrounding her. But that would more than shock him. He'd think she'd gone completely daft.

Yet the urge was strong enough she couldn't quite trust herself to remain in control. So she turned away.

Chapter Eleven

atthias couldn't deny the pleasure of the evening spent with Opal's family. Her cousin was more outspoken than Opal but had a likeability that made her questions not seem impertinent. And Ezra's easygoing ways blended with his wife's temperament perfectly.

And Opal. He'd been content to watcher her hold the babe all evening, snuggling and cooing. Her eyes shone every time she looked at the child. She was made to be a mother. Just being near the bairn seemed to make her glow, and 'twas from more than the firelight shimmering from her face as she now rocked the child.

"Will you be leaving in the morning then?" Ezra's words drew Matthias away from his focus on Opal.

But the question seemed to grab her, too. She looked up, her eyes finding his. Did she seem…troubled? But of course she wouldn't want to leave her family yet.

"We can wait a few more days, if you like." He could do his hunting in this area for the Yule feast. Maybe come back to the Reid home each evening and feast his eyes on Opal while she smiled at that baby.

She offered him a soft look, although not as happy as she'd given the child. "No. We should go tomorrow. I need to get back to Mountain Bluff."

He searched her eyes. Surely Mutti and Vatti could wait a few more days. They'd allow anything she asked.

Yet her look seemed resigned. She nodded at him, still holding his gaze, and the corners of her mouth pulled up. "I've already packed us a lunch. Would you prefer first light?"

She would insist then. Still… He shook his head. "We can wait a couple hours for the sun to warm." And that would give her a little more time to enjoy her family.

After all, family was a treasure people didn't fully appreciate until it was gone.

Perhaps getting a late start had been a bad idea. Not only had Opal cried when they left—although she'd tried to hide it from him—she'd barely spoken more than a handful of words the entire first half of the day. Perhaps he should have insisted she spend more time with her family. But the parting had to come at some point.

They'd skirted the towns of Atlantic City and South Pass, then stopped for a few minutes to eat the lunch Opal had packed. He should be thankful for her silence. Thankful she didn't chatter on like some women. But this quiet hung thick with a sadness that ate at him like a wolf at a deer carcass.

Maybe he could get her talking to pull her from her thoughts. "Did I ever tell you about the time my great, great ancestor Brandur was almost killed by a six-year-old boy?"

"No."

He glanced at her out of the corner of his eye. "The lad's name was Egill, and they were in the midst of a week-long game meeting. Apparently, the boy was still smarting from being bested earlier in the day. Grandfather Brandur was in the midst of a rousing game of Knattleikr. He'd just thrown the ball when Egill charged up to him and slammed an axe into the back of his head."

Opal gasped loud enough to catch his horse's attention. Both of Karl's ears turned toward her, and he shook his muzzle.

"You must be jesting. How could a little boy be so violent? What had they done to incite him? Was the boy punished?" The horror in her tone sent a frisson of unease through him. Perhaps such a gory tale wasn't the best to draw her out of her gloom.

"I don't know all the details exactly. That's the only part I can remember my father telling."

"Did he live?"

He cut her a glance. "My father?"

She sighed. "Your ancestor."

He shrugged. "I'm sure he died at some point. Things were pretty brutal back in those days."

She narrowed her gaze at him. "How long ago did this happen?"

He tilted his head, pretending to calculate the number. "Must be about a thousand years."

She blew out a breath. "You're exasperating some days, Matthias Björk. And here you had me thinking your great-grandfather was a savage brute."

He shrugged again. "He might have been. My father told lots of stories of the olden days. I wish I could remember them all."

She lapsed into silence again, and he waited. Maybe she would volunteer a tale of her own.

But she didn't. Another half hour passed with nothing but the sounds of their squeaking saddles and the birds in the trees above. They still traveled the Oregon trail, although the fork toward Mountain Bluff should be nearing in another mile or two.

If he and Karl were alone, they would take advantage of such an even path for galloping. Maybe Opal would enjoy a romp, too. He slid a glance at her. At least she didn't ride side-saddle. She'd be able to hang on at a decent canter. And she handled the horse well.

"You up for a race?"

"Beg pardon?" She swiveled to look at him, her brows knitting as though she thought she'd misunderstood.

"A race. This stretch is flat enough, and Karl needs to stretch his legs. We'll go easy on you. Just say the word when you want to stop."

Her brows returned to their normal position, even though her eyes narrowed. "Doesn't sound like much of a race."

Oh, ho. She had a feisty bone, it seemed.

He let one corner of his mouth pull up. "All right. We won't go easy on you. But we'll still stop any time you call out."

She looked down the road, which curved toward the left in a gentle arch so they could only see a couple hundred feet ahead. "If I remember correctly, there's a butte that breaks the tree line on the right up ahead. Whoever's in the lead when we reach it shall be crowned the winner."

Crowned, eh? But he wasn't about to argue the point. Instead, he pulled Karl to a stop and motioned her to rein in beside him. "On the count of three, we'll begin."

She nodded.

"One. Two. Thre—" The first sound of *three* had barely touched his lips when her gelding leapt forward.

He pressed his calves to Karl's side and leaned low as his gelding lunged forward. He could have easily had taken the lead had both animals started at the same time. As it was, a full horse length separated Karl's muzzle from Butter's streaming tail.

119

Karl's massive stride was closing the distance, though, as they rounded the curve in the road. He caught up with Butter's rump, charging hard while the scenery whizzed by.

The rock butte had come into view ahead as Karl's nose pulled even with Opal's stirrup. She glanced sideways at them and squealed, then leaned lower. Her gelding surged forward.

Matthias yelled encouragement to his gelding as the wind pulsed through his hair, lighting a fire in his veins. This was the kind of excitement that made him feel truly alive.

Karl edged closer to the lead, but the little bullet Opal rode had more speed than he'd given him credit for. As the rock wall flew by the edge of his vision, the bay gelding still led by a nose. Or maybe less.

Opal sat up and slowed her horse, and Karl eased his speed at the same time, even though Matthias couldn't bring himself to rein him in.

The horses slowed to a trot, and a soft laugh rang from the woman on his left. He glanced over, not even trying to hide his grin.

The smile that split her face as they settled into a walk made something flip in his chest, which caught his breath. The sun's rays framed her profile from behind, making her shimmer just like the angel she was.

He couldn't help a bit of teasing, anything to keep that smile on her face. "I think we won, especially given the fact you cheated."

Her laugh tinkled out like the clearest bell. "Cheated? You said to start on three, and that's exactly what we did. Butter and I won quite fairly."

A smart little minx. He only shook his head.

Opal inhaled deeply of the cool mountain air, then let the last of her sadness drain away with her spent breath. She'd not felt so alive and invigorated since…well maybe since the last time she'd been galloping through the countryside with this man. Although 'twas quite a bit more comfortable to have her own horse instead of clinging to the back of his.

She glanced over at him, sitting tall astride his steed. "You seem to make a habit of taking me on wild romps through the mountains, Mr. Björk."

He gave her a grin that bordered on devilish, yet it set off a chorus of flutters in her midsection that felt all too good. "I'm only showing you fun you might not have experienced before."

This man had the ability to make her feel so alive. 'Twas as if he knew exactly what she needed and how to bring her up from any level of despair.

She gave him her full focus, and he met her gaze squarely. "Thank you. I appreciate it more than you could know."

The smile grooves around his eyes and mouth softened, and he gave a single nod. "I'm glad."

An easy silence settled over them, and she chanced the opportunity to ask a question. "Did you hear any news of your sister while you were gone?"

He sighed. "Nothing encouraging. A few replies came from people who'd never seen her."

How hard that must be for him, to know his sister was out there somewhere, but he couldn't reach her. "So, what next?" But a part of her dreaded his answer. Would he leave them again? Of course he would. Mountain Bluff wasn't his home, or at least not any more than the rest of the mountain wilderness. The real questions were where would he go and for how long?

"Well..." His voice came out strong, matter-of-fact. "When we get back to Mountain Bluff, I'll deposit you at the boardinghouse and go hunting."

"Hunting?" For his sister?

He bobbed his chin in a solid nod. "For a wild boar, if we're lucky. We need a good ham roast for Yule. If we're not so favored, though, we've been known to enjoy a good venison roast almost as much." He cut a wink in her direction.

"Yule? You mean Christmas?"

"My ancestors' version of the holiday. Except we drag it out over twelve days of feasting and games, starting a few days before Christmas and going into the new year. A Viking Yule is not an experience to miss."

"What kind of games?" The feasting she could imagine, what with the amount of food Mrs. Shumeister

122

cooked. But it took a moment to imagine this man playing whist or dominoes or game of the goose.

"Well, the sagas talk about games like wrestling and swimming competitions, and of course, Knattleikr." He sent her a sideways glance, which spurred the memory of his earlier story.

"You mean the game where little boys attack grown men with axe blades?" Sounded perfectly barbaric, these ancient people.

His mouth quirked. "That's not always how 'twas played, from what I've read."

That grabbed her interest. "You have books that tell of these games from a thousand years ago? Are they your family's books passed down from one generation to the next?"

"The writings aren't from my family, but they are sagas written by Icelandic Vikings of old, like the Grettis saga and the Egills saga. I do have a few things that have been handed down through my family, though." He reached up to his collar and fiddled with the buttons of his coat. They seemed to give him trouble, so he removed his gloves and worked at the fastenings with weather-roughened hands.

She couldn't help but watch him, although he hadn't said what he was doing. Perhaps he meant only to scratch at a rash that plagued him. The thought was enough to pull her gaze from him as a surge of heat flooded her neck.

"This is one of my heirlooms."

She turned back as he extracted a pendant from under his collar. The metal piece hung from a leather thong and formed the shape of a cross. She reined in her mare, and he did the same so she could lean closer to examine it. "Look at that scrollwork in the metal," she said. "Was that carved, do you think?" The detail was remarkable, even though the pendant bore some rust and obvious wear.

"The design was pounded into it, more likely. This type of metal only gives at very high temperatures."

She leaned closer to touch the scroll-work, careful not to let her fingers brush his skin as he cradled the treasure in his palm. "How old is it?"

"I'm not sure, to be honest. But this design was used mostly in the tenth and eleventh centuries. And that would explain its condition."

"Remarkable." Exhaling a breath, she stole a glance up at him. She hadn't realized how close they were, with her leaning toward his horse. Less than a foot separated them, and the warmth of his breath brushed across her face in a way that sent skitters down her arms.

It would only take a small movement on his part to close the distance between them, should he want to take her in his arms. Or kiss her.

The thought scalded her like a jab from a red-hot fire poker, and she jerked backward, ramming her spine straight as she gathered her reins. She didn't dare look anywhere near his face. Had he read her thoughts at all? Heaven help her.

124

Surely he wasn't clairvoyant. Although he did seem to have unusual perception at times.

She clamped her lip between her teeth to hold in a groan. What had she been thinking? Other than what it might be like to feel the strength of his arms around her. What would his kiss be like? Honestly, she'd never had a pleasant thought about a kiss, not after all Tori had endured at the hands of Father's steward. Both of them had sworn they'd never trust a man.

But then Tori found Ezra, which opened the possibility to them both that decent men did exist, albeit one had to search far and wide to find them. Or more likely...God would have to make the match, if He had such a thing planned for her.

And it certainly wouldn't do her any good to become swoony about this man, who'd offered only to accompany her on a short journey. Her guardian, of sorts. Although, she didn't like the thought of being under his authority. Power seemed to easily puff up a man's self-opinion.

Would Matthias be the same way? He had such a frank humility about him, almost as if he didn't think of himself at all, and certainly not enough to hold a high opinion of his worth. Dependable. That's what came to mind when she thought of Matthias Björk.

She stole a glance as he rode beside her. Handsome, too. But that thought, like so many that had passed her mind in the last few moments, would only get her in trouble.

Chapter Twelve

atthias watched Opal across the flickering light of the campfire as he munched the dinner she'd laid out of smoked buffalo meat and reheated flapjacks. He probably should have gone hunting tonight, but they'd waited too late before stopping to camp. He didn't mind the dry fare, but it certainly wasn't as rich and flavorful as the food she cooked in Mutti's kitchen.

She was a riddle, this woman. Such a beauty, with her elfin features and that thick, long braid didn't much conceal how soft her hair must be. And those eyes. In the dancing firelight, they darkened to a sapphire blue.

"Are you thinking of your sister?"

He straightened. He couldn't tell her what he'd really been thinking. Not out here with just the two of them. Already, they'd spent far too much time alone. People didn't judge about such things in little remote villages like Mountain Bluff. But he wasn't naïve enough to think their situation would pass as anything close to proper if it took place back east. They both knew the bounds of propriety, and hinting at his current line of thought would take a perfectly innocent journey to a place he had no business going.

So, he nodded. "Alanna's always near my thoughts."

She played with the bottom edge of her coat. "You said she's older than you. What does she look like?"

"You, actually."

She straightened, as though not quite sure how to take the comment.

"As best, I can remember, she had long blond hair that she always kept braided. I think blue eyes, but then other times it seems like I remember green."

She cocked her head. "I was born and raised in Pennsylvania."

Did she think he meant…? "I didn't mean to imply you were my sister, Miss Boyd." Heaven's no. Even the thought made him want to breathe a sigh of relief that it couldn't be so. "Only that I noticed the resemblance that day I first met you."

"The day your horse fell in the creek?" She said it with a light tone. Teasing.

"I suppose that's why it took me a moment to gather my wits while you helped Karl out of the water."

She raised her brows. "I see. I'd assumed you'd bumped your head on the rock. That was the only way I could account for your behavior on the ride back."

He straightened. "My behavior? You were so sullen and disagreeable, I had to do something to pull you from your foul mood."

"Foul mood?" Her tone rose more than a little. "I'll have you know, sir, I'm known far and wide for the sweetness of my disposition. I'm never in a *foul mood*."

A statement he fully agreed with, but he wasn't about to admit it. And he was enjoying too much the sight of her as feisty as a Greek goddess, the flames dancing in her fiery gaze.

So, he took his opening and returned another thrust. "Of course, my lady. For your current mood could only be considered as sweet as a sugar delight."

She opened her mouth to respond, but no words spewed out. Closing her lips, she narrowed her gaze at him. "Touché, Mr. Björk. You've won the point fairly."

For a moment, the way her mouth pinched made him want to take back his last comment and anything else that might have offended. But then the corners of her mouth quirked, as though she were holding in a smile. "I must say, that was almost as invigorating as racing through the countryside."

Oh, she was too fair for words when her eyes danced like that. He'd be in trouble if he sat here watching much longer.

So instead, he pushed to his feet and brushed the crumbs from his hands. "I'm going to check the horses. Go ahead and get some sleep."

If he spent long enough out in the cold and darkness letting the Almighty settle his thoughts, maybe the Lord would also see fit to put her to sleep before he returned.

Surely that wasn't too much to ask. After all, a man could only handle so much before his defenses slipped.

Matthias laid another log on the fire the next morning, darting a glance at the sleeping woman while the flames crackled and popped as they licked at the dry wood. Her sleep seemed deep enough to last until he had this Pheasant cooked.

Had the ride yesterday exhausted her so much? It well could have done, especially since she wasn't accustomed to riding horseback all day. And two weeks of caring for her cousin's household, not to mention the new babe, had likely played a part.

Extracting his knife from its case at his side, he whittled a point in the stick he'd found for roasting, then pierced the raw meat and raised it over the flame. He could set up a spit so he didn't have to sit and hold the meat while it roasted, but the quiet time would be nice. He'd already done the morning chores, so this would give him a chance to organize his thoughts and center them where they belonged—on the Lord.

His gaze wandered to the sleeping woman. Despite the fact that she was obviously so competent in the kitchen and running a household, she had a vulnerability about her. As though she'd rather be invisible than noticed. Was that her nature—a God-given part of her personality? Yet her timidity seemed more rooted in fear than anything. And Scripture even said, *For God hath not given us the spirit of fear; but of power, and of love, and of a sound mind.*

What in her past had planted her fear? He'd have to watch for hints about it.

A half hour later, the meal was ready. Maybe 'twas the aroma of fresh-cooked meat, even though he had no herbs to enhance the flavor, but just as he pulled the perfectly roasted Pheasant from the fire, Opal's eyelids fluttered open.

For a second, her sleepy gaze seemed to hover, seeing everything yet not focusing. Then her eyes flew to his face, sharpening. She sat up, and a yawn captured her mouth in the cutest way as she turned aside to cover her face.

He looked away, too. She was too beautiful for words, especially in times like this.

As he busied himself dividing the meat, she slipped away into the woods. He poured fresh coffee for them both and was enjoying his first sip as she reappeared, looking much more awake than she had a few minutes before.

"I'm sorry I slept so late." She scanned the area. "What can I do?"

He lifted her tin mug of coffee. "Sit and eat. We'll ride out after we finish."

She ate quietly, but the silence hung easily around them. Companionable. As she finished her meat and corncake, she offered a soft smile. "That was excellent. Thank you."

He shrugged. "Not as good as what you make."

She pulled her coat's hood up to cover her head and ears. "I never thought I'd so appreciate the value of a warm meal on a cold winter morning."

Within minutes they were on the trail and covered ground easily through the first half of the day. As they mounted up again after lunch, he glanced around at the familiar landmarks. They would be back in Mountain Bluff within a couple hours, and this might be his last chance to learn more about her past.

The trail wound through rocky terrain as they made their way up, down, and around a cluster of low mountains. That meant he was in the lead and wouldn't be able to see her face as she spoke.

If she spoke.

And how should he go about asking? Just come out and say, *Opal, I get the feeling you've had a hard life. Anything you wanna tell me about?* Which begged the question…Why in the whole mountain territory did he want to know? He was supposed to make it his goal to stay away from close friendships, so others wouldn't suffer from the overspray of his impulsive decisions. He should simply keep his mouth shut and save this woman the angst.

Yet something inside prodded him to know her better. Maybe this was one of those very impulsive decisions that seemed to hallmark his life. But he'd never been good at spotting them from the front end. He shouldn't expect to change that now. He pressed forward before he could stop himself.

Turning in his saddle, he flashed her a pleasant expression and forced a casual air. "You know about the scattered remnants of my family. What of yours? Are your parents still in Pennsylvania, checking daily at the post office for word from you? Any brothers or sisters left behind to take over the family holdings?" Because 'twas obvious she'd been raised among refinements he could never imagine. Which only piqued his curiosity more about what could have sent her all the way across the country to this uncultured wilderness.

An emotion flashed across her face, but she cleared it so quickly, he couldn't be sure what he'd seen. Especially not with him twisted in the saddle and the rocking of both horses' gaits, making it hard to focus.

Her expression took on a guarded look. "My mother died when I was born, so I have no siblings. My father is still alive, quite aptly running the family holdings for himself."

"Back in Pennsylvania?"

She nodded. "Riverdale is his estate." She spoke of it as if she had nothing to do with the place or with him.

"Is that where you grew up?" If she gave another clipped answer, he'd relent. She could share the details when she was ready. When she felt she could trust him.

Her eyes took on a sadness that made her look far older than her age, and she nodded. "Tori lived there with us, too, after her parents left. She was like a sister, my closest friend."

At last. Her cousin seemed to be a safe topic from her past. "I can tell the two of you are close."

"She's always been there when I needed her, even though I haven't always been able to return the favor."

What did that mean? A well of history in that statement, he had no doubt.

She glanced up at him. "Did the Shumeisters tell you of our adventure when we first came to this territory? After Tori left Mountain Bluff to follow Ezra back to the stage stop?"

She was trying to change the subject. Letting him know he'd pushed far enough. But at least she'd not shut down the conversation entirely.

"Don't think I've heard that story." Neither Vatti nor Mutti would have retold anything they thought private. They knew the value of trustworthiness, even though they knew him to be capable of holding a confidence. At least, he prayed they felt that way.

"My father's steward came after us. He hired a local man to help kidnap us, and they caught Tori after she left Mountain Bluff. Ezra had already come back to the stage stop to pick me up so we could join Tori at the boardinghouse. We found her horse partway."

He'd reined Karl to a stop at the word kidnap and listened to the story unfold, bile churning in his gut.

She met his gaze now with a melancholy wistfulness. "About the spot where we started racing yesterday, the horse came cantering from the woods, saddle and reins flapping, but no Tori."

133

The churning in his gut thickened, creating enough pressure to ignite a spark in his veins. "What then?"

"We followed the tracks all night and halfway through the next day. Finally found them holed up in an abandoned cabin. Jackson had strangled Tori until she was unconscious, but at least she was able to recover after Ezra saved her."

Matthias simply stared as his mind followed the story, circling until he'd picked up on all the pieces she wasn't saying. "Jackson was your father's man?"

She nodded.

"And where is he now?"

"Dead. The killer he hired couldn't even stand the depths of his evil nature. He shot Jackson as he was about to kill Ezra."

And now the question that was searing his insides. "Did your father know his employee's wickedness?"

"He must have. I shared my own concerns more than once." Her voice had taken on a harder tone. "Not as much as I should have, though. I should have pushed harder. Made him believe me and do something about it so Tori didn't have to endure such things."

Now the hardness in her voice shifted to an ache that made him want to cradle her in his arms.

He did his best to keep his tone gentle. "Sometimes when a person doesn't want to see something, no amount of pleading can make them believe."

She looked like she might cry. "But I let Tori down. She suffered atrocities no proper person should imagine, much less speak of. And I had the power to stop it, if I'd only had the courage."

He turned his horse so he could face her directly. "You didn't let her down, Opal. Your father did, if he even suspected what was happening and took no action. He let you both down."

She raised her chin a notch, but then her teeth caught her lower lip, as if she were holding in emotion. The last thing he wanted was a crying woman on his hands. But even more than that, he didn't want her to experience one more moment of pain from any of the men who'd hurt her in the past.

Nudging Karl forward, he reined him beside Opal's mare so the horses stood nose to tail. From this spot, he could be within easy reach of this woman. Close enough for her to read the determination in his face. Her skirts brushed his leg, but he did his best to ignore the sensation.

"You needn't ever fear that man again, Opal. And if any other man worries, bring that concern to me. Please. I promise I will take action. I will not let you be hurt again. Even by your father."

Maybe he shouldn't have tacked on that last part, but he had the feeling the man could easily bring her pain, whether physically or to her tender heart.

Tears glistened in her eyes as she met his gaze, but, blessedly, they didn't fall. She nodded and sniffed—delicately—just like the lady she was.

Now he had to find a way to make sure he was always near enough to make good on his promise.

Chapter Thirteen

As they reached to the boardinghouse door, Opal allowed Matthias to open it for her. Before she could even step across the threshold, the click of dog paws on wooden floors sounded and a yellow muzzle nosed around the door.

"Charmer." She dropped to her knees and took the dog's sweet head in her hands, then rested her cheek against him as he pushed into her. "I missed you, too, boy."

She breathed in the comforting scent of him, and would have stayed in that position much longer if it weren't for the shuffle of Matthias' boots on the boardwalk behind her.

She rose to her feet, but kept a hand on the dog's head while he tucked himself against her skirt. As she moved inside, the kitchen door opened and Mrs. S. charged toward them. "Oh, lieblings. You're home."

Opal sank into the warm embrace as the woman enveloped her. She'd never known a mother's warm, soft embrace could soothe a person's insides—at least she'd not known it before meeting this special lady. She pressed her eyes shut and returned the hug. "'Tis good to be home."

Mrs. S. pulled back and studied Opal's face for a long moment. What did she see in her scrutiny? How much Opal had enjoyed spending time with her family? Or maybe she could see the hidden part inside that was thankful to finally be home. But surely she didn't see that deeper place that seemed to have healed since she'd told Matthias about her father.

Nay, maybe healed wasn't the word. Lifted. As though a weight smothering a portion of her heart had been pulled away, freeing a lighter part inside her. Whether Matthias really meant it or not, he'd offered to champion her. She'd never take him up on it, of course. Lord willing, she wouldn't need to. But he'd offered. If only for that moment, he acted as if she were worth his effort.

"Ja. Dinner is ready. Come and sit while I put it on ze table." Mrs. S. turned and motioned for Matthias to follow them but kept hold of Opal's hand. This touch felt so motherly, she wouldn't have pulled her hand away for all the world.

But in the dining room, Mrs. S. released her grip and motioned for Opal to her usual place. "Sit and rest. You are weary from your travels. Gunther will be in soon, and ze doctor is in his room. We all sit and eat together."

"But I can help you bring the food in." She was weary, yes, but it wouldn't feel right to sit while the older woman worked.

Mrs. S. waved the words away as she turned. "Wash and sit."

As their host disappeared, Opal glanced at Matthias. Would he think her weak to rest instead of working as she was paid to do?

But he only motioned toward the wash basin against the wall. "After you."

She followed his direction and could feel the strength of his presence as he waited his turn behind her. He wasn't standing too close, nor did he seem impatient, but she'd suddenly become very aware of him.

After drying her hands on the cloth, she turned and offered a shy smile. "Your turn." What was wrong with her that she suddenly couldn't look him in the eye?

Thankfully, footsteps lumbered down the stairway, and Doctor Howard appeared, saving her from making a complete ninny of herself.

"The travelers have finally returned, I see. I suppose Gunther's gone to kill the fatted calf?" The doctor's tone was chipper, which meant business must have been light for the day.

She returned his smile. "Mrs. Shumeister won't even let me help in the kitchen."

He nodded. "As it should be. Now sit and tell me about your family. They're all in good health, I believe your telegraph said? And you have a niece?"

As she started in on the news, Mr. S. arrived and stopped the conversation to hug Opal and shake Matthias's

139

hand. Mrs. S. bustled in and out from the kitchen, carrying platters and trays until the table overflowed with warm and savory foods.

At last, they all sat for Mr. Shumeister to speak the blessing. His simple heartfelt words always left her feeling blessed and nurtured, even though they were meant for the Lord, not for her. Maybe 'twas the fact that prayer made this mismatched group feel like family. Well, mostly. The Shumeisters, anyway. And perhaps the doctor was like an uncle.

And Matthias? No matter how she tried, 'twas impossible to relegate him to the role of brother. But best she *not* try to imagine what role she'd like him to fill.

After the *amen*, she scanned the table, then slid a glance to the man who'd once again taken over her thoughts. He caught her look with raised brows, and she made her eyes round and innocent. "Is this like the feasting you talked about during the twelve days of Yule?"

"Ja. Yule is coming." Mrs. S. pointed toward Matthias. "You are going hunting?"

He nodded. "I'll leave in the morning."

She looked to Opal. "We start cooking tomorrow."

Opal nodded. "I'm ready." And as the conversation flowed around her, the warmth in her chest grew with each passing moment. How good it was to finally be home.

Matthias ran a hand through his still-damp hair as he stood outside the kitchen door, then wiped his palms on his buckskin pants. He had no reason to stand here staring at the door. He should go in and gather the food bundle the ladies would have prepared, then get on his way. He only had three days left to find a wild hog and get back for the first night of Yule.

But he knew for a fact Mutti wasn't inside that kitchen, as he'd just passed her going out the back door. And from the sounds of industry drifting through the door, Opal must be in there, kneading dough or mixing flour or doing who knew what else. He'd spent days alone with her, so why did he dread these few moments as he gathered his pack and took his leave?

If he'd quit lying to himself, the answer would be clear. He didn't want to leave. This woman had become far too important to him.

And that was exactly why he'd best grab the food and high-tail it into the mountains. He squared his shoulders. He was too much for anyone to be saddled to, and certainly not someone as sweet as Opal Boyd. She needed someone safe, someone who would live a quiet, settled life with her. Someone who could be counted on to keep her out of trouble. And that someone could never be him. He knew exactly what he was. Not safe. Not quiet. Not settled.

He'd have to put some distance between them, for her own good. And his. He'd said he would protect her, but what a foolish thought that was. He could never be anybody's protector.

Gripping the handle, he pushed the door open and stepped inside.

Opal looked up from her usual place at the work counter, and the soft smile she offered made something tighten in his chest. "Good morning."

He looked away. "I'm headed out. Mutti sometimes packs food."

"Right here." She moved to the table, the swish of her skirts almost ringing in his ears. "I added in some cookies I baked this morning. You may want to try one while they're still warm."

The smile in her voice forced him to look at her. She was so blasted pretty, with that petite nose and cute little pointed chin. And those eyes.

He tore his focus away, then reached for the bundle. The rough cloth settled in his palm, and he closed his hand around it.

"Do you know how long you'll be gone?"

He'd thought he did. But maybe he should rethink his plans for Yule. Tell Mutti on his way out that he wouldn't be back with a boar. She could use the rest of the ham from the hog they butchered in the fall. He would spend a quiet week in Jackson and celebrate Christmas with the locals there. Although, quiet may not be the word for their version of the holiday.

142

The silence hung heavy in the room as Opal waited for his answer. "I don't know. I'll be back when I'm back." She had to know he wasn't dependable. To understand that he couldn't be the solid, steady man she needed.

He spun on his heel and headed toward the door. With any luck, she'd be glad to see him go.

Opal listened to the retreating boot thuds as Matthias stomped down the back hall. Then the sound faded into the crackling of the fire in the cook stove.

That wasn't the same man she'd ridden beside the last two days. Not the same man who promised he would not let her be hurt again. Even by her father. Not the same man who'd looked at her so tenderly just yesterday.

What had happened to change him? What put that cloak over his gaze to keep his thoughts from showing in his eyes? She'd seen that kind of expression before. Tori could shield her thoughts and feelings in the same way, keeping them from displaying on her face. Had done it so many times back at Riverdale, Opal could spot the reaction at a glance. Usually when she feared getting too close to what was really happening. Afraid she was about to be hurt. Or had just experienced pain.

Was Matthias afraid of getting hurt? But that didn't make a bit of sense. Maybe 'twas the opposite. He was such a good man, perhaps he thought she was growing feelings for him, and he meant to warn her off. That would make sense, given the way she'd been acting toward him.

But she wouldn't develop an attachment to him. She intended only…friendship. How could one spend day after day in another's company and not feel kindly toward that person? After all, he was so…noble and kind and honest and…good. Worthy of someone much more special than her.

Mrs. S.'s heavy tread puttered through the dining room, forcing Opal from the gloom of her thoughts. She was late getting the bread in the oven, which meant it would put all of them behind this morning.

"Well. Zat man. He says he may not be back for Yule. I don't understand." She propped her hands on her ample hips and shook her head, her brows knitting as though she were looking for the hidden meaning behind Matthias's words. "It doesn't make sense."

"Perhaps he's traveling to make more inquiries about his sister." She should keep quiet, yet the words slipped out as she loaded the oven full of bread pans. It wouldn't do for the Shumeisters to think ill of him just because he was trying to protect her feelings.

Although, if she'd realized at the time what he was doing, she'd have let him know she had no intention of developing affection for him or any other man. She was doing just fine living out her days here in this little kitchen.

Mrs. S. harrumphed. "He knows I'll make Christmas stollen. He'll be back."

The words almost pulled a smile from Opal. Food was always the answer for Mrs. S., whatever the problem might be. Cooking was the gift she gave those she loved, which meant Christmas was likely to be a flurry of food.

Gifts.

Opal almost dropped the cup of flour she'd just scooped from the bin. She'd not even thought about gifts for the holiday, had nothing to give the Shumeisters on Christmas morning. How had she missed that? Probably because Father had always frowned on any form of holiday celebrations. Each year, she and Tori would try to do a kindness for the staff—most of them anyway—but nothing like the real Christmas gifts the other girls at school would flaunt.

But this year would be different. The Shumeisters had come to mean so much to her, she had to do something to show them her appreciation, at least in a small way. And Matthias. If by chance he did come for Christmas, if not for the whole twelve days of the Yule holiday he'd talked so much about, he deserved something special.

She had a few dollars put away. A trip to the mercantile was in order after the morning baking.

As Opal reached for the mercantile door later that morning, an unusual scent caught her attention. Something like a mix of horse and cologne water. Not a very appealing blend, but definitely one that stood out. She glanced around the street and boardwalk, but the place was surprisingly empty. Even the anvil was silent at the livery across the street. The hair on the back of her neck stood up, as though something were wrong. Or maybe someone was watching her.

But perhaps that was all her imagination. She gripped the door handle and slipped inside the store.

Chancelor's mercantile seemed as warm and inviting as it always did, with rows of foodstuffs and supplies broken up by the occasional display of more frivolous niceties.

When she told the man her reason for coming, he reached under the counter and pulled out a shallow tray. Black fabric covered most of it, and in the center sat an elegant ruby brooch, a glittering display of beauty.

"Any woman would be pleased to receive such a gift. A true sign of regard." Mr. Chancelor's voice hummed low and reverent, as though he'd given the speech more than once. A jewel like this was likely not easy to peddle in this remote town.

She offered a patronizing smile. "I'm sure. I've never seen Mrs. Shumeister wear a brooch, though." And with the cost of this one, it would take all her savings. Which she would happily spend if she really thought her friend would want the piece. Somehow, though, it didn't seem like the right gift for sensible Mrs. S.

But what would be? Something useful like a new pair of knit gloves? Or maybe the fur-lined leather pair. They would be harder to work in but keep her hands warmer if she stayed outside. Perfect for a horseback ride into the mountains.

Although Mrs. Shumeister didn't ride. In fact, Opal had never even seen her climb into a wagon. They walked around town or into the woods to find herbs. The knit gloves would be better for gathering plants.

So...perhaps the gloves.

She made her way around the perimeter of the store, pausing at the wall where all the tools hung. Would Mr. S. want something from here? Or perhaps a good book. The mercantile only carried three volumes. An almanac. A novel called *Great Expectations* by a fellow named Charles Dickens. *A Popular Cyclopedia of Modern Domestic Medicine* by Keith Imray. They already had a doctor in the house, so that last one shouldn't be necessary. The novel might be an interesting diversion for Mr. S.

Now, Matthias. Should she purchase anything for him? If he didn't come for Christmas, she'd feel more than foolish giving it to him later. Or she could simply send it to Ezra instead. Which reminded her, she should ship Tori a Christmas present, as well.

And now she needed something for Doctor Howard. Mayhap the medical tome. A smile pulled at her cheeks.

She didn't have to decide it all right then, but she only had a few days left to make ready.

Chapter Fourteen

atthias crept through the trees, arrow notched in his bow as he scanned the underbrush for movement. The cloven-hooved tracks were fresh, so the herd of wild hogs couldn't be far ahead of him.

There. In the dim, early-morning light, the flimsy branches of a low cedar wiggled. A black body rubbed against it, snout raised to the air as the animal caught the breeze. Exactly why he'd been careful to stay downwind from them. Hogs seemed to have remarkable sense of smell. A wonder that they could have any ability left after smelling their own stench, but 'twas a fact.

He raised the bow and took aim. Though he had his pistol strapped at his waist, he preferred to use his bow for easier prey like this. It kept him in practice. The animal at which he now aimed was a smaller boar, so he'd do best to get a clean chest shot. The animal would still be aplenty for the Yule feast at the Shumeisters.

The hog turned and seemed to sense Matthias there. The distance was perfect. He focused again, then released the arrow.

A whistle, then the thwack of the point hitting its mark. The animal's squeal split the morning air as it jerked. More squeals sounded, and the rest of the herd broke through the underbrush, scattering in all directions.

He kept his focus on his target. The pig with the arrow leapt in a circle, then turned and darted almost head-first into a tree, shifting to the side at the last second.

Matthias pulled another arrow from the quiver on his back. Perhaps, the first hadn't hit its mark exactly. The other pigs still squealed in a terrible ruckus, but he forced out all sound that could distract him.

He fitted the notch against the string, but a force slammed into him from behind. It knocked him forward, and he scrambled to keep himself upright, but the brute kept pushing. He tried to throw the bow and arrow to the side, but the tip caught on the ground, tangling in the bow and his arms.

He fought to free his hands to brace his body as he slammed into the ground. His shoulder landed on sharp point even as something hard and heavy hit the back of his leg.

A pig?

He twisted to see a black form charging again. "Yah!" He kicked out at the animal, catching its snout with his boot and turning it away.

"Get!" He kicked again, but the animal seemed to have spent its fury as it ran squealing in the other direction.

The sounds of screaming pigs faded into the distance as he sank back against the ground. His breath came hard and quick as his pulse still surged in his neck. That was the first time he'd ever been attacked by a pig.

A grunt sounded about a dozen feet away, and he jerked his head up. Had the boar come back for another go? But no, the pig that had first been his prey lay there, an arrow shaft sticking from its chest. Apparently, he'd hit the right mark.

Bracing his hands on the ground, he pushed himself up to a sitting position. His head went light as a wave of dizziness slammed him. His shoulder and neck throbbed something awful, too.

As the spinning ebbed, he glanced down at his bow and arrow on the ground where he'd lain. The bow appeared unscathed, but the arrow had snapped in two. His shoulder may have caused that damage. His coat had protected his skin, but he reached up to rub the part of his neck that still stung.

His hand came away bloody. Feeling the cut again, it seemed to be just that—a cut from the notched end of the arrow. Not deep enough to require stitches, and no spurting blood that would mean he'd injured a vein.

Unbuttoning the top three loops of his coat, he peeled back the right side to check his shoulder. No blood showed on his shirt. The thickness of the deer hide had probably protected his skin from the arrow penetrating.

He rubbed his neck again. More blood, but he'd live. After gathering his things, he pushed to his feet. The dizziness flooded back, making him stumble, so he reached for a tree to steady himself. He'd left Karl back where he first saw the hog tracks, so he'd best go back for the gelding and his tools.

Then 'twas time to go to Mountain Bluff. He'd debated for four days now, but he couldn't quite force himself to stay away. Mutti would expect him.

The last thing he wanted to do was hurt her feelings intentionally. He did enough of that without trying. And he'd promised Opal he would show her the excitement of Yule. Of the promises he'd made her, at least that one he could keep.

"Come, boy. You can help me dump the wash water." Opal held the back door with her body while she balanced the bucket of used water in one hand and the lantern in the other. Charmer ambled out, taking his own sweet time. He paused to sniff at the snow that lingered on the ground, then stepped gingerly on it. She resisted the urge to nudge him forward so she could shut the door. "Tis not as bad as all that."

Leaving the dog behind, she strolled to the edge of the yard where the wood began. The lantern cast a halo of yellow light, forming deep shadows in the boot prints scattered across the clearing. There were only a few inches of snow left, but they were likely to get another layer any time.

Today was the first day of Yule, and Matthias hadn't come to celebrate. That shouldn't leave her with such an ache in her chest. She and Mrs. S. had been cooking and baking since yesterday, and they'd all enjoyed a hearty feast tonight. The Shumeisters and Doctor Howard had been here, and the Chancellors from the mercantile had even come to join them. The table had been full enough, it'd not been obvious they were missing a person.

Yet that person's absence had left a greater hole than even his broad frame should be able to fill.

She set the lantern on the ground so she could dump the bucket, then raised the light again and looked around. This was just about the spot where she'd found Charmer, and at about this same time of night, although the moon had been much brighter then.

"You remember this place, boy?" She shifted the lantern to the hand that carried the bucket, then reached down to scratch the dog behind his ears.

He leaned against her skirts, tilting his head up in doggy appreciation.

But then his ears pricked and he straightened, staring off into the distance.

"What is it?" She followed his gaze but couldn't see anything other than darkness outside of the light.

But then a sound met her ears. The shuffling of something in the snow. Animal or man?

152

"Who's there?" Her voice came out too wobbly, probably because her pulse pounded like a beggar at the door.

"Opal?"

"Matthias?" She almost sagged in relief. "What are you doing out there?"

A large form took shape in the darkness, too dark to recognize the figure on top, but she'd know that white-gray steed anywhere.

Matthias reined in the horse, and she set her bucket and lantern on the ground so she could step forward and stroke the gelding. "Hey, boy."

Behind her, Charmer let out a bark as if to remind them of his presence.

"Hey there, pup." Matthias's voice sounded weary.

Her eyes roamed up to take him in, a shadowed giant with his fur hood pulled up to cover his head. "Go on inside. I can put away this boy, and Mrs. S. will be so glad to see you. We almost gave up on you coming."

He leaned forward, and for a moment, it looked like he might fall off the horse in a heap. But he caught himself with the saddle horn and slid his legs down to meet the ground. "I'll see to Karl. I have a wild hog for the celebration, too." His voice seemed to slur, as though he were…intoxicated? No, that wasn't right. He'd never imbibed, not even the brandy the saddle maker had brought when Mr. S. had been injured.

Maybe the slur came from exhaustion. She gathered the horse's reins and used her no-nonsense voice. "You must be tired. I'll see to things."

153

He still had a hand propped on the saddle, as though he needed it for support. "All right." The weariness in those two words made her want to slip herself under his arm and let him lean on her as he struggled inside. Would he even make it on his own?

But he straightened and turned to the bundle behind his saddle. She moved around to the other side and unfastened the strap there. It was a roll of leather, and, from the smells emanating, it must contain that pork he'd mentioned.

When they had it loose, Matthias heaved the bundle on his shoulder with a grunt.

"Can I help you with that?" Her instincts screamed to run around the horse and take at least one end of the bundle. She probably couldn't have carried the whole thing, which meant it might be too much for him in this exhausted state, too.

But he trudged forward, weaving a little under the load. Yet his stride held an air of his usual determination.

She turned back to the gelding. "Well, Karl. You must be weary, too. I'll bet we have a nice bucket of oats for you."

A quarter hour later, she had the gelding settled in the little shed where Matthias usually stabled him. One might wonder why he hadn't taken the horse to the livery, where accommodations would surely be more comfortable for such a big animal. Yet that day when she and Matthias had left to visit Tori had made the reason very clear to her. Mr. Lefton would sooner point a rifle at him than stable his horse.

With Matthias's pack over her shoulder and her hands full of his bedroll, as well as her original bucket and lantern, she and Charmer headed for the house.

The dining room was quiet, and as she rounded the corner, only Mr. S. sat in his chair. "Where's Matthias?" Had he already retired for the night? Sure, he'd been exhausted, but he must need to eat. And she'd not even had the presence of mind outside to wish him a Happy Yule, or whatever one said to celebrate the holiday.

"He's gone to settle in his room. Do not fear, he'll be back to eat." Mr. S. nursed a mug as he offered a gentle smile. His blond mustache covered much of the curve of his mouth, but the twinkle in his pale blue eyes was unmistakable.

From the looks of the heaping plate in front of Matthias's usual seat, Mrs. S. had been insistent about that. And just now, the older woman probably needed help in the kitchen. Would she work on the pork tonight? Probably, since mornings were so busy with baking.

She turned toward the kitchen door. "I'd best go help Mrs. S."

"Nein. Come and sit, liebling. Our boy will want to tell us about his trip while he eats."

She paused, every part of her wanting to obey his suggestion—could it pass for a command?—but she was being paid to help, not sit. "Maybe I can relieve Mrs. S. so she can come and visit. I know she'd like to."

"Nein." This time the word was definitely closer to an order. He almost never took that tone, but it left no doubt he meant for her to listen. "Sit and visit." He motioned toward her chair across from Matthias's place.

She sank into it. Yet sitting idle felt so wrong. Especially since Matthias wasn't even here yet.

Thankfully, his boots sounded on the stairs. Slowly. As though every step took great effort.

He rounded the corner into the dining room, and she found herself rising before she could stop. His blond hair was slicked back as though he'd just washed his face, the golden stubble on his jaw much thicker than when he'd left five days ago.

But what drew her focus more than anything else were those dark shadows above his cheeks, as though his eyes had sunk deeper into their sockets. Had he not slept since he left them?

"Sit and eat." She motioned toward his plate as she moved to the tea pot to fill his mug. "I hope you're hungry. I think Mrs. S. gave you a heaping portion of everything."

He sank into his chair and paused for a second to stare at the food. Was he saying a silent prayer? Savoring the aroma? It actually looked more like he was gathering his strength before he reached for his fork and stabbed a slice of meat.

"You look tired. Are you feeling all right?" She couldn't help but ask. She'd never seen him in this condition, and it had tied a ball of nerves in her stomach.

"Rode straight through since yesterday morning. Just need a few hours' sleep."

156

"You rode all night? Why?" He'd done this to himself? He was practically ill. She couldn't imagine a single reason worth pushing so hard.

He looked up, and his expression might have been sheepish if he hadn't looked so hollowed out. "I was trying to get back for the first day of Yule."

If that didn't beat all. She sank into her chair. "Happy Yule, Mr. Björk."

One corner of his mouth tipped.

"Is there specific tradition for this first day?" She glanced from Matthias to Mr. S., then back to their weary traveler.

"Normally, we eat a lot and tell a few stories from years past. Years way past, like the sagas of old." His mouth tipped again. "Maybe I'll save that part for tomorrow."

It made her chest ache to see him like this. So exhausted that eating alone seemed to use all his energy. But he surely needed the food. If he hadn't stopped to sleep, he probably hadn't eaten more than jerky and stale biscuits.

She glanced at Mr. S. "I'll look forward to it tomorrow. For now, I'd best go see if I can help Mrs. S. in the kitchen."

They worked together for a while, preparing the meat Matthias had brought so it would be ready to cook the next day. Then Opal started her final clean-up. "You go on out and visit with the men now." She motioned toward the door.

"Ja. I will." Mrs. S. patted Opal's shoulder, then removed her apron and left the room.

It only took another moment before Opal had the kitchen tidy. Her ears strained to pick up on the voices humming from the other room, but no words were decipherable. If only there were something she could do to help Matthias. But after food, he probably needed sleep more than anything.

Chapter Fifteen

pal stepped through the doorway just as Matthias rose from his chair.

"Gute nacht, son," Mr. S said. "Sleep well."

Matthias nodded to the older man, then stepped toward Mrs. S. and planted a kiss on her cheek.

"Schlaf' gut, mein liebling." She patted his arm.

Opal had to swallow down a lump in her throat. *Sleep well, my love.* She knew those simple German words. Had heard Mrs. S. say them in her most tender moments.

Matthias straightened and turned to Opal, weariness cloaking every one of his movements.

She couldn't help a soft smile. "I'm headed upstairs, too. I'll walk with you." From the looks of him, he might need her to catch him if he collapsed along the way.

He nodded.

She said her good-nights to the older couple and fell into step behind Matthias. At the bottom of the stairs, he motioned ahead. "After you."

Part of her didn't want to take the lead. He looked like she might need to stay behind to soften his fall. But she followed his direction and took the stairs ahead of him.

She couldn't help glancing behind as she climbed, couldn't help but notice the way his hand gripped the rail with each step. His knuckles white as though he were pulling himself up.

At the top, they reached his room first, and she stopped. "I'm glad you came back." She could chastise him for pushing himself when one night of sleep wouldn't have hurt anything. But that wouldn't help him just now, and his effort should be acknowledged. Thanked.

He nodded. "I wasn't planning to, but the farther away I went, the more I wanted to be here. By the time I changed my mind, I was several days ride away." In the lantern light, his face seemed to soften, drawing her closer before she realized she'd taken a step.

"Thank you. It means much to us all to have you here."

What was that expression that crossed his face? With the shadows, she couldn't make it out. Especially when his features softened again so quickly.

"Opal, I..." He paused, and that expression came again.

She raised the lantern to see him better. But a dark line on his neck grabbed her focus. Was that...blood? "What happened to you?"

She closed the distance between them and reached to touch the spot. Blood dried over a nasty cut.

"'Tis nothing. Just a tussle with a hog when I was hunting."

She raised her gaze to his face. "A hog did this to you?"

His mouth pinched. "Well, that cut is actually from an arrow."

She raised the lantern even higher. "An Indian arrow?" She'd not actually seen Indians in these parts, but she'd certainly heard stories.

He chuckled. "Nay. A Viking arrow. My own, but the story is long enough to wait for tomorrow."

She traced the cut again with the tip of her finger. "This needs to be tended. Are you hurt anywhere else?"

His hand closed around hers. "I'm fine. It doesn't hurt at all."

Every breath stilled. Every thought fled her mind as she looked up into eyes that seemed to soak her in. Eyes that she could lose herself inside.

His other hand brushed her cheek, then settled there, its warmth bringing to life every part of her.

Yet still, his gaze held her in place. Until it lowered— just a little—to her lips. Was he going to kiss her? What kind of heaven that might be.

His face moved nearer, the steady warmth of his hands holding her secure—one on her cheek and the other holding her hand at his neck. Yet she wouldn't have moved away. Couldn't think of anything in life she wanted more than this kiss. Right now.

Her eyelids drifted closed as his lips brushed hers, the touch washing through her like warm liquid on a cold day. She barely recovered from the sensation when his mouth returned. This time she was ready and greeted the touch with a boldness she wouldn't have thought she possessed. Yet she wasn't prepared for the charge of lightning that reached all the way through her.

Sweet mackinaw. She was more delicious than he'd ever let himself imagine. He shouldn't be kissing her. Not here and now. Not ever. But when she'd touched his neck, the sweet scent of her filling his head, he'd lost his last thread of strength to withstand her.

And now, the way she kissed him back, he couldn't regret it.

This woman. Opal. The one whose strength he'd come to admire more than any person he'd let himself spend time with. She was not only good and strong and prettier than a mountain lake in full sunset, but she was here. In his arms. Kissing him back.

He forced himself to slow the kiss. To pull back, before he lost every bit of his good sense. She trusted him. And he wasn't altogether sure he had the strength to keep from breaking that trust if he let himself go much farther.

With effort, he pulled back an inch, yet that was as far as he could go. Resting his forehead on hers, he breathed in the warmth of her breath, the feel of her skin under his hands. The essence of her.

"Matthias." His name on her lips came out breathy, as though she were struggling to pull herself together, too.

He inhaled deeply, then eased back a little more. At least enough that he could see her face better, although the shadows from the dim lantern light shaded most of her features.

Yet even now, she was so beautiful. The way her blond hair feathered away from her face, that dainty pointed chin. Those eyes. They stared at him with an intensity that stirred a fresh longing in his chest.

He brushed her cheek with the pad of his thumb. "I shouldn't have done that. I'm sorry."

She held his gaze. "I'm not."

Sweet hotcakes, but she was almost more than he could withstand. He straightened and gathered strength to back away. But her mouth beckoned for one final brushing. Heaven.

He did step back this time, stroked her cheek with his thumb once more, then relinquished his grip on her hand. "Go get some sleep."

"Good night." She gave a soft smile then slowly turned away and padded down the hall to her room.

Hopefully she would be able to sleep. It would be a long time before his pulse slowed enough to rest. No matter that he'd been awake for two days.

Opal stepped through the back door as a whiff of cold air blew in with her. Charmer charged inside, too, weaving right in front of her in that bothersome manner he'd recently begun. "Move, boy. Out of the way."

He did shuffle to the side, but only after his wagging tail flapped against her skirts, tangling them in her limbs.

After finally shifting past the dog, she scurried forward. Mr. S. needed more supplies for his roasting of the pig in the yard, and he was waiting for her.

As she pushed into the kitchen, the sight there sent her skidding to a stop. Matthias stood beside the stove, hip propped against the work counter, one foot cocked. He held a mug of coffee in one hand and looked at her with his mouth tipped in a way that melted her all the way through. His face still sported a field of blond stubble, yet his green eyes were clear and bright…and giving her that look.

"Good morning." She worked to pull herself together, to ignore the way every part of her reacted to him. Especially to that roguish smile.

Stepping farther into the room, she scanned her scattered thoughts for what Mr. S. had sent her for. A serving platter. Tongs. Fire poker.

"'Mornin'."

And just like that, his sleep-roughened voice made her stomach twirl and every thought slide out of her mind. She peeked up at him and met that rich gaze. "Did you sleep well?"

The contented, almost self-satisfied look on his face gave the answer for him. But he nodded anyway. "Feel like a new man."

Did their kiss have anything to do with that? Or maybe it hadn't meant as much to him as it had to her. The way her pulse stuttered, even now, as the memory flooded back through her.

She dropped her gaze from his. "Mr. and Mrs. S. are outside roasting the pig. I just came in to retrieve a few things."

"I'd best go out and see where I can help."

She reached for the cloth covering the plate she'd set aside earlier. "Sit and eat first."

"Do you have time to join me?" Did he sound hopeful, or was he just being nice? The last thing she wanted was for him to think he needed to patronize her just to solace her feelings.

She inhaled a sharp breath but didn't meet his gaze. "I need to take these outside. They're waiting for me."

"All right. I'll be there shortly."

And with that, she escaped out the door. Hopefully, she'd gathered what Mr. S. needed. Because she'd not be going back while Matthias loitered here.

Maybe 'twas Matthias's imagination, but Opal seemed to be avoiding him. All day, when he entered a room, she found a reason to leave it. Or else she buried her focus in her work. And now, as they sat around the hearth in the great room after dinner, she'd taken the chair farthest from him and kept her eyes glued to her sewing.

Was it possible that kiss hadn't meant as much to her as it had to him? She certainly didn't seem like a woman who gave her affection away freely. In fact, quite the opposite. She'd kept herself distant from the very beginning. Which should have been a blessing. He should have left it alone.

But he'd never been one to back down from a challenge. And quite honestly, he couldn't bring himself to regret last night's kiss. Not with Opal. 'Twas getting harder to deny how special she was. Special enough that he should get himself far away from her. For her sake.

Yet a growing part of him just couldn't bring himself to leave.

"Matthias, tell us one of your sagas." Mutti sat beside her husband on the sofa, working on her on own sewing, but she looked up over the rim of her spectacles as she spoke.

"Any particular one?" He had the perfect story in mind, but first he'd play along so it wouldn't be obvious how much thought he'd put into this.

"Anything you choose."

"All right, then." He squinted as if he were trying to recall a tale. "Many years ago, back when the Vikings still warred to increase their kingdoms, stories were told of Odin who traveled the world on his flying, eight-legged white horse named Sleipnir."

He glanced at Opal. Her head was cocked like she was listening, yet she kept her focus on the fabric in her hands.

"Odin led the Wild Hunt, a group who would fly over villages and countryside, delivering toys and candy. Children would fill their boots with straw for Sleipnir and set them by their hearths. Odin would slip down chimneys and fire holes, leaving his gifts behind for the good children. For those that hadn't been so good, he left them a lump of coal."

"And where did he get the toys and candy?"

He smiled at Mutti's prodding. She'd heard the tale before, so she must be prompting for Opal's sake.

"His elves made them. Everyone knew he was lord of Alfheim, home of the elves who dwelled deep within the earth. They loved their master so much, they worked all year to make magical toys and candy for him to give out. And of course, the coal."

That finally earned him a glance from Opal. A rather dour look, but he'd take it. He returned a grin and a shrug. "I'm just telling the tale as it was said to me."

"This eight-legged horse must have been something, indeed, to carry toys to all the Viking children." Her tone was overly wondrous, almost patronizing.

He nodded. "Indeed. A favorite among all the children."

"Hmm…" She turned back to her sewing, yet a little smile remained at her mouth.

And that was exactly what he'd been working for.

Mutti was the next to tell a story, the one about Sankt Nikolaus who kept a record in his book of which children were good, then brought them candy and treats on Sankt Nikolaus Day.

'Twas always fun to hear the different stories about Christmas traditions, but they all knew what was coming next as Vatti reached for the Bible on the table beside his chair. Or...at least he and Mutti knew what was coming. Opal looked on with interest, that small smile still touching her mouth.

"The fables are fun to imagine, but lest we forget the greatest gift..." He flipped a page, then skimmed the text with his finger. "Here we are. 'And it came to pass in those days, that there went out a decree from Caesar Augustus, that all the world should be taxed...'"

The old familiar story soaked through him like a warm blanket, even as little nuances seemed to come alive. He could almost see the glory of the Lord shining around the shepherds, and the way that sight must have startled them. What might it have been like for plain, working-class men to be visited by God's messenger? To be part of the Christ child's story?

Too soon, Vatti finished the section and closed the book. He reached to take Mutti's hand. "I zink I'm ready for sleep. Ze morning comes soon."

She smiled back at him, giving a little glimpse of what she must have looked like as a young woman, in love with her Gunther.

"I'm ready to retire, too." Opal tucked her sewing in the basket beside her chair, then rose, taking the lantern she always carried upstairs. "Good night, all."

He bounced to his feet before he could stop himself. "I'll walk you up." After a quick good-night to the older couple, he took long strides to catch up with Opal. She'd certainly not waited for him.

Nor did she look back as she ascended the stairs ahead of him. If she meant to ignore him, she'd be disappointed. Maybe that kiss hadn't affected her, but it had brought something to life for him. Could she mean to pretend it never happened? He had to find out. Even if asking made him more vulnerable than he liked. He'd not meant to kiss her, but now he had to do something about it.

Chapter Sixteen

When Matthias reached the upstairs hall, Opal was only one determined step ahead of him. "Opal?"

She showed no sign of stopping, so he reached for her arm. "Opal, wait."

She spun. "Maybe you should call me Miss Boyd."

He tried not to wince at the verbal slap, but at least she now stood listening. "Miss Boyd, then. I need to say something."

She didn't answer, and the angle of the lantern left her face in shadows. Yet he could see the rise and fall of the lace at her collar as she took hard breaths.

"Last night, I'm sorry if I offended you. But…I'm not sorry I kissed you." Was it his imagination or had she gasped? Well, she'd better lace up her boots because more scandalous things were a'coming.

"I don't know if you've felt this thing between us, or maybe 'tis all on my end." He paused for a response—anything from her. He'd even take another gasp at this point, but nothing from the shadows. *Lord, what am I doing?*

170

Like the irrepressible fool he was, he charged on. "What I'm trying to say is, I'd like to spend more time with you. To see if there's something that could be more. Than friends, I mean."

Opal fought back the burn of tears. *He'd meant the kiss?* The whirl of emotions that had surged through her all day seemed to be culminating in one overwhelming wave. His words couldn't be true. He couldn't really be here saying he wanted to be more than friends.

"Won't you say something? Even if you hate the idea, please tell me."

She jerked her gaze up to his, the hint of…fear?…in his gaze giving her a sudden boost of courage. She even had to bite back a bit of a smile. "I can't believe you said that. I didn't think the kiss meant anything to you. I was trying to put some distance between us. To make it easier for you to pretend nothing happened."

He ducked a little so he was nearer to eye-level with her. Maybe so he could see her face better in the shadows. She raised the lantern, letting the warm light spill across his features.

"I thought as much. And…I can't promise I'm any kind of catch." He pressed his lips together, and his brows lowered. "Actually, getting close to me can sometimes be a bit dangerous, or at least painful. Maybe you should run while you can."

Those brows scrunched together, and her fingers itched to smooth them. Could she? Did she dare? It wouldn't normally be proper, but…maybe if he were courting her.

Before she lost her nerve, she stretched up and pressed her first two fingers to his left brow, smoothing along its surface. The wrinkle in the other brow melted away at the same time, and he tilted his head so his cheek pressed into her palm.

With that tiny motion, the shadow of scruff on his face tickled her skin and sent a shiver all the way down her arm. He turned his head a little more and pressed a kiss into her palm. Sweet, warm taffy. That shiver spread through her entire core, so strong she had to press her eyes closed just to control her reaction.

"I probably shouldn't make a habit of these hallway meetings, but if your answer is yes, I'll find other places to entertain you. More suitable places."

"Yes." The simple word was all she could manage, but she finally forced her eyes open to drink him in.

He sank another kiss into her palm, then lowered her hand. "Good night, then."

"Good night." But 'twas another moment before she could force herself to turn and walk down the hall.

"Go on, you rascal." A couple days later, Opal pushed Charmer's nose away from the cedar tree for the third time. But he edged right back, intent on whatever animal smell he'd picked up. As he craned through the feathery needles, several ribbon decorations fluttered to the ground.

"That's it. Out of here." She stepped between the dog and the tree, grabbing her skirts in both hands and flapping them. "Git. Shoo."

A deep chuckle sounded from the other side of the tree, but its owner didn't come any nearer to aid her cause.

Charmer finally seemed to get the message, though, because he turned and trotted away. His tail wasn't exactly between his legs, but it didn't wave quite as high as usual.

She turned back to the tree at the edge of the Shumeisters' rear yard, sending Matthias a glare.

He returned the look with an unrepentant grin. "I think you hurt his feelings."

"He keeps knocking the decorations off. We'll never finish if he wallows in the branches, undoing all our work."

"You know he'll just bide his time and come back when we're gone. And likely bring a host of animal friends."

She did her best to defend against that hint of a smirk on Matthias's face. The rogue. But one glance at him slashed through her fortifications. She bit down on her lower lip to keep at least some of her grin inside. Goodness sakes, but he was handsome, with that tilt of his mouth bringing out the strength of his jawline and his noble cheekbones. But it was that softness in his eyes that melted her all the way to the core.

173

Still, she couldn't stand here and stare at him all day, no matter how much she'd like to. With effort, she pulled her gaze away, sending a quick glance at Mrs. S., almost hidden by the girth of the evergreen. Thankfully, the woman wasn't paying them any notice as she arranged a bow on one of the branches. Did she realize something was different between her and Matthias? Hopefully they weren't that obvious, despite the way the air almost crackled anytime he looked at her.

They passed another half hour in peaceful quiet while they worked. Although not exactly quiet, as the forest sounds settled over them. The call of a mourning dove. The chatter of a squirrel.

"Oh." Mrs. S. broke through the peaceful blanket. "I just remembered I set aside a crate of dried berries to use on zis tree. The doctor put zem in the upstairs closet, I believe."

Matthias stepped back, his gaze scanning their work on the evergreen. "I'll get it. Are there markings on the box?"

"Just William Barr and Company."

He nodded and caught Opal's gaze. That smile again. And the way his green eyes sparkled, 'twas enough to heat her all the way through.

After he'd gone in the house, she stepped over to the crate of carved wooden ornaments and selected a star shape. "Here's another angel. I thought we'd hung them all." She turned and held up the elaborate carving for Mrs. S.

The woman nodded, but she seemed to be staring at Opal, not the ornament.

174

Opal returned the look with raised brows. Something must be troubling the older woman.

"You are happy with Matthias, ja?"

She couldn't help the heat that flamed up her neck, and she turned toward the tree to find places for the decorations. If Matthias intended to court her, it would be clear enough to the Shumeisters soon. She might as well ease them into it. "I do like him. He's a good man." She chanced a glance at the older woman, who was still watching her with the beginnings of a smile tugging her lips.

"Ja. He is. He only needs to know he is loved just as God made him."

Loved. The word had slid through her mind as she waited for sleep the night before, but she wasn't ready to speak of it with anyone yet. How could she even know for sure what love felt like? Or maybe 'twas more than a feeling.

"Miss Boyd."

Opal spun at the bark of the man's voice. "Mr. Lefton?"

The livery owner strode toward them from the direction of the street. With each determined step, his body seemed to radiate anger. And something long dangled from his hand. A pack of some kind? Too slender to hold much.

But as he came within a dozen feet, the shape registered in her mind with startling awareness. An arrow quiver.

Lefton's face had mottled red under his winter beard, and he didn't seem to know whether to focus his attention on her or Mrs. Shumeister as he planted himself a half-dozen feet from the tree.

He raised the leather case so the fringe hanging from the bottom waved in the air. Something else dangled with the strips. Feathers.

"Can you tell me, either one of you fine ladies, why your dog would be carrying around an Indian arrow case?" He seemed to be working hard to contain his fury, although his words fairly dripped with sarcasm.

"My dog?" She peered closer at the item. Some kind of beadwork or painting adorned the body of the case. 'Twas a beautiful piece, really. And it definitely looked to be made by an Indian. "Are you sure Charmer brought this? Where would he have gotten such a thing?"

He impaled her with a look so venomous it took everything in her not to wrap her arms around herself for protection. "From an Indian, Miss Boyd. Or perhaps from an *Indian-lover.*" He coated those last words with pure hatred, and Opal did grip her elbows this time, bracing them as a barrier between her and his rage. She'd never imagined he harbored such poison.

But she worked to keep her voice solid and her chin up. She would cower to no man. "I'm not sure what you mean, Mr. Lefton. If 'twas my dog carrying such a thing, he must have picked it up in the mountain somewhere. Are you concerned about Indians attacking us?"

His eyes narrowed to beady slits. "Why would Indians attack you, Miss Boyd. You have one of them practically living with you."

Living with...? She turned to Mrs. S. to see if she had any idea what the man meant.

Mrs. Shumeister's face possessed its own glare, and she'd turned the force of it on the livery owner. "Henry Lefton. It's time you speak plain."

"All right. You want plain? Matthias Björk is a murderer and a savage. When he's not sponging off your good graces, he's off with his Indian friends killing good people and stealing their life possessions."

Opal inhaled a breath so sharp it nearly choked her. Yet she couldn't focus on anything other than the words hovering in the air like a cloud of acrid smoke. A murderer? He'd muttered a few insults about Matthias when she was leaving to visit Tori, but she'd assumed the man was grumpy from the cold.

Yet this was no flippant mention. This insult was a direct affront. But Lefton knew nothing of Matthias. How dare he make such accusations?

Stepping forward, she leveled her own glare on the man. "Mr. Lefton. Apparently, you've been misinformed. Mr. Björk is neither a murderer nor a thief. He is the best of men." *Better than you.* But she knew better than to push her luck by speaking that last bit aloud.

177

He matched her step forward and held up the leather quiver, practically shaking it at her. "Are you trying to tell me this isn't what he carries his arrows around in?"

She examined the pack again. It didn't look familiar at all. Yet Matthias did have a bow and arrows. He used them for hunting. He'd said so himself. Yet if this were his quiver, 'twas not because he went raiding with Indian cohorts. There was no doubt of that in her mind.

She turned her ire on the man again. "I have no idea if it belongs to him. And, frankly, it matters not. Matthias would never hurt a man or animal for sport, nor take what isn't his." With every word, fire burned hotter in her veins. "If you have something against him, I suggest you settle it with Matthias directly. I've had more than enough of your insults. You will not besmirch the good name of Matthias Björk. Do I make myself clear?" She'd never spoken to a man like that, yet the flames still surged through her chest. She'd do more than yell, if necessary, to stop this scoundrel from damaging Matthias's reputation.

But the rage on Lefton's face seemed to ease at her words. Or maybe it wasn't easing so much as shifting into a look so cold and calculating, it slid a shiver down her back.

"You think so highly of him, do you?" He took another step forward, only a couple feet separating them now.

Yet she could almost feel the power of his arms around her, strapping her hands to her sides, smothering her so she couldn't get away. Couldn't save herself from him. The feeling wrapped around her throat, cutting off her air and stopping any sound from escaping.

"That's quite enough, Heir Lefton." Mrs. S. used her no-nonsense tone.

"I'll say it is." A new voice. *Matthias*. He must have approached from behind Lefton, where the blacksmith's bulk hid him from view.

She was torn between a relief strong enough to pull all strength from her limbs and the urge to yell for him to get away from this monster. This man meant him harm, and her paltry statements weren't enough to stop him.

Matthias stepped toward Mrs. S., bringing himself into full view of the man. "'Tis time you leave, Lefton. Whatever your trouble with me, it doesn't involve these ladies." His voice had taken on an edge of steel, a competence that made her want to cheer. Or sob.

Mr. Lefton, of course, turned his focus to Matthias, allowing her the chance to step away from him. Matthias edged in closer, creating a kind of barrier between her and the angry man.

Lefton's temper hadn't abated any. He flung the quiver on the ground at Matthias's feet. "You act so noble, but you're nothing more than a savage." Smoke seemed to erupt from his ears, although that may have been his breath in the cold air.

He looked ready to hurdle another insult at Matthias, but then he clamped his mouth shut and spun away.

After stomping a few steps, he turned back, apparently unable to keep his parting blow inside. "You'll pay for your sins, Björk. I'll make sure of it."

Chapter Seventeen

atthias had to get Opal alone. Mutti had kept her occupied all afternoon like a mother hen corralling her brood, but he had to find a chance to talk with her. Find out what kind of damage that half-brained smithy had done. The man's words were a bunch of idle tripe, but Opal wouldn't know that. Not for sure anyway.

Not that him defending himself would give solid proof. It would just be his response to the accusations. But at least he could find out what she now thought of him. And suddenly, Opal Boyd's opinion of him mattered far more than anything.

Pushing that thought down, he peered around the open kitchen door. "Anyone want to help a poor fellow gather holly? We'd better get cracking if we plan to have wreaths for Christmas tomorrow."

Mutti looked up from her work at the table. Her expressions were once hard for him to decipher, what with the way she always looked so no-nonsense. But when he'd realized that twitch of her cheek was the way she concealed a smile, she'd become as easy to read as an open letter.

Just now her cheek pulled the slightest bit. "Opal, are those rolls ready for ze oven now?"

"They are." Opal turned to face them, raising her arm to brush away stray hairs with the back of her wrist.

His hands itched to tuck those strands back himself. Maybe sink his fingers deep into the rest of her hair. He knew from experience 'twas soft, but his memories weren't as good as real life.

The awareness of her gaze seeped through him, and he met those eyes with his own. He couldn't stop the little smile that pulled at his mouth. "Does that mean you're free to help?"

Her gaze flicked away from his—to Mutti. Perhaps he shouldn't be pulling her out of the kitchen on such a busy baking day, what with Christmas tomorrow. But she needed a bit of fresh air. And he needed desperately to talk with her.

And if it happened that she didn't believe the rumors about him and was willing to share in a pre-Christmas kiss, well…all the better.

"Ja, go gather holly. We're late making the wreaths." Mutti waved them away, her cheek twitching, even though she wouldn't meet his gaze.

After Opal had bundled in her coat, scarf, and gloves, they set out on the trail behind the house. The nearest holly tree wasn't far, but perhaps he could take a more winding path to get there.

He wore his fur coat and buckskin gloves, but his hands found his coat pockets for extra protection as a gust of wind whipped up.

"So why are we on a holly-gathering expedition?" Opal tucked her fingers through the crook of his arm, securing herself close to him with her other hand. Too bad his bulky covering blocked much of the feel of her.

He slowed to a stroll. Maybe he could stretch this outing until the chill of the sunset forced them to return. If only…

But he forced his mind away from that line of thought and onto her question. "We're cutting holly to make wreaths."

"I gathered that much. But how did these holly wreaths come to be such an important part of the Yule celebration?" She turned her face up to him.

Her face shone in the winter light, with those elfin features tucked into the scarf she'd wrapped around her ears. He had to keep himself walking or he'd lean down to kiss that pert little nose. Or those soft lips.

She looked away then, maybe because she could read his mind. Or maybe because she thought one of them should look where they were walking.

But it gave him a chance to let out a long breath and clear his mind. Holly. Right. "Holly was a favorite with the Vikings. Because it stays green through the winter, it reminds us that life continues. And we make them into wreaths, which symbolizes to the way each season goes into the next, making

183

the circle of the year. So, a holly wreath is basically a reminder that winter will eventually end and spring will come again."

"Hmm..."

'Twas hard to tell if her *hmmm* was thoughtful or if she was just plain bored. He'd probably overdone it a bit with the explanation. Who really cared about the meaning behind holly wreaths anyway? He had more important matters to discuss.

But he had to be careful about how he broached the topic. "Opal, when Lefton came earlier..." How did he say this exactly?

"That man makes me so angry." Her body stiffened against his side. "I don't know why he thinks those things about you, but he has no right spouting them off to anyone who will listen."

Maybe he shouldn't have been so concerned. "I can't figure the reason behind his strange accusations. 'Tis not like he really knows me, only what he might have heard from the Shumeisters or someone else around town."

"Has he ever been civil to you?"

"Not once. Not even the first time I stopped to leave Karl with him. He nearly chased me off with a pitchfork."

"Hmm..."

Again with that same vague response. But this time 'twas easier to think her *hmm* meant she was mulling the problem over. Was she pondering whether he really was innocent of the man's charges? After all, most accusations had at least some root in truth. Surely she harbored at least the

184

shadow of a doubt about him. He had to know for sure. After all, he'd never been one to shy away from facing something that bothered him.

"Do you wonder if he's right?" He kept his tone soft, gentle. Not betraying the tightness in his throat that threatened to strangle him.

She looked up at him again, and he had to force himself to meet her gaze. She needed to see he had nothing to hide. Yet if he saw doubt in her eyes, it would be torture to watch her good opinion of him falter.

She seemed to study him for an interminable moment. Or maybe she was trying to find the right words. Words to let him down gently.

At last, she spoke. "I think the entire situation is strange, I'll grant that. But nothing Lefton or anyone else could say changes what I've seen with my own eyes. From the way you care for the Shumeisters as if they were your own parents, to the way you proved yourself more than a gentleman when you escorted me to visit Tori. And a host of other moments it would take me hours to describe. You're a good man, Matthias Björk. I've seen that."

Her words brought a lump to his throat that stopped any response he might have summoned. She was wrong. He wasn't a good man, no matter how much he longed to be. But he wasn't about to clarify that for her. Not when Opal Boyd looked at him with those luminous blue eyes. And that soft smile curving her sweet lips.

She seemed to realize that he wasn't ready to answer. Breaking their locked gazes, she stepped forward, pulling him with her. When had they stopped walking? "Come. We're taking the long way to the grove of holly trees, but 'tis right up here."

They'd cut enough holly branches to fasten ten wreaths, at least, before Opal finally allowed Matthias to turn them back toward the boardinghouse. Evening was falling fast, which meant she was overdue to help with dinner, but this time alone with him had been the best Christmas gift she could imagine. And the thought of gifts reminded her she'd probably be up late that night finishing his. It would be worth it, though, as long as he liked her simple offering. *Lord, let him like it.*

Matthias fell into step beside her, carrying the lion's share of their load.

She'd taken the conversation deeper than she intended on the first part of their walk, so it would be best to speak of happy things on the return trip. "So I think I know what happens on Christmas day. What other delights do I have to look forward to for the remainder of Yule?"

"Well." He reached to snag a holly branch slipping out of his bundle. "Mostly more of the same. Lots of food, games, and stories. Sometimes we can get Vatti to play a few tunes on his violin."

186

She turned to stare at him. "He plays an instrument?"

He gave a firm nod. "Not unless we can talk him into it, but he hides a great deal of talent. Not that he'd admit to it."

She turned her focus back to the rocky trail. "Hmm…" Life was ever full of surprises.

"Also…" Something about his tone made her turn back to him. Matthias sent her a glance filled with enough apprehension to tighten a knot in her stomach.

"What?"

"I received word today from someone who may know where my sister is located."

"That's great news." The knot started to uncoil inside her. His look must be just the nerves of his mission finally being so close to fulfillment.

He nodded, but the hesitation in the action and the way he cut another look at her pulled those nerves tight again in her midsection.

"The wire came from the Montana Territory. It said she's left the town, but I need to go there and see if I can find out where she went."

It took a moment before the full meaning of his words soaked in. The Montana Territory was weeks away, depending on where exactly he would be going. Not a journey to take lightly.

But this was one step closer to something he'd been working toward for a long time now. Family. "That's great." She sounded like a mockingbird, repeating the same phrase over and over. Drawing in a breath, she tried for something new. "When will you leave?"

The warmth of his gaze heated her cheek, but she didn't turn to look at him. Couldn't. Or he might see the sting of tears scalding her eyes. 'Twas not as if he weren't coming back. Or maybe that's what he was trying to tell her.

Now she had to look at him, to gauge his answer to the question she had to ask. "Do you...think you'll be back?"

"Opal." He stopped now, turning to face her fully. His hands came up to cup her arms, making her wish his gloves and her coat didn't separate them so fully. But the tenderness in his dark green eyes was the next best thing to a caress. "I'll be back. I need to see if Alanna is still near that town. I may need to track down a few leads. But I'll be back. Hopefully before the spring thaw."

Before the spring thaw. An eternity from now. She nodded, her gaze dipping to his chin so she didn't have to look in those eyes again. Her tears burned too close to the surface.

A long breath eked out from him, as if he didn't want to leave any more than she wanted him to. But that wasn't the way he should feel. This might very well be the trip where he would find his sister.

Straightening her spine, she raised her chin and forced herself to meet his gaze. "Go to Montana. Find your sister. Then bring her back so I can meet her."

The edges of his eyes formed crinkles, highlighting the twinkle inside them. "Yes, ma'am." And then he lowered his mouth and pressed a soft kiss to her lips. Sweet. So tender. A simple meeting of hearts.

He pulled back and gave her one of those grins that made her chest flip. "We'd best get back. The Yule wreaths won't make themselves."

Chapter Eighteen

Christmas Day passed in a blur of cooking and feasting, and by the time they gathered around the fire that evening, Opal's body ached from all the activity. Not to mention that she'd overstuffed herself with Dresdner stollen. An interesting recipe Mrs. S. said had been handed down through five generations of her family's women.

But now…now was the moment she'd been preparing for. She shouldn't be nervous. Either these people would like her gifts or they wouldn't. She shouldn't let their opinions be so important to her.

The Shumeisters handed out their gifts first, hers being a new apron embroidered with an elegant rose and her name. Then the doctor's turn. He'd given her lovely writing paper and one of those new fountain pens she'd heard about before she left Riverdale. Had he ordered away for it? Very thoughtful.

Matthias motioned for her to go next, and she first pulled out the packages for the Shumeisters. Mrs. S. gushed over the gloves—a paltry gift, and it made her almost wish she'd gotten the brooch, too.

But when the dear woman wrapped Opal in a tight embrace, she murmured, "Danke, liebling. You're the best gift I could ever have." And that brought a smile to Opal, even through the tears that threatened again. She'd never been so emotional in her life.

Mr. S. opened his book next, and gave her such a wide grin, her heart threatened to melt right in her chest. He stepped forward and planted a kiss on her cheek, his bushy mustache tickling in a way that made him all the more dear.

"Your turn, doctor." She handed him a package of candies—his favorite licorice—and he offered his own kiss on her cheek. Good thing the room wasn't bright enough for them to see her blush. So much attention centered on her.

Finally, she turned to Matthias, fully aware of all three pairs of eyes watching them. He had that twinkle in his eyes, and the flickering light from the fire made the stubble on his jaw glisten.

She handed him the simple brown, paper-wrapped package. He took it, a smile curving the corners of his mouth.

His fingers looked large and a little clumsy as he found the slit and peeled back the edges of the wrapping. The green wool of the scarf peeked out.

Her gaze wandered up to his face as he lifted the gift she'd spent the last several nights knitting. Was that disappointment that flickered across his face? Maybe just her nerves imagining things.

191

As he fingered the fringe at the edge, he looked at her, his lips meeting in a warm smile that eased the knot in her middle. "You made this?"

She nodded, melting into the tenderness of his gaze.

At last, he shifted his focus back down to the gift again, still fingering the yarn. Then he reached for his own pile of small packages. These were wrapped in an indigo cloth that reminded her of the skirt material Mrs. S. had been working with a few weeks before.

He handed his gifts out at the same time, but Opal held her small, flat bundle while she watched the others. Mrs. S. gasped as she unfolded the cloth edges, the clatter of wood bumping against wood drawing everyone's attention.

She held up the outline of a bird. A cookie cutter? "They're lovely, Matthias. You carved them?" She raised another outline, this one a tree. Then a heart.

He nodded, and Opal leaned closer to see the remaining shapes in the box. The detail was exceptional.

"*Sind schön.* Lovely." Mrs. S. leaned forward then and pulled Matthias close enough to kiss his cheek. "Merry Christmas, liebling."

'Twas hard to tell in the dim light, but Matthias's face seemed to grow a few shades ruddier.

The doctor opened his next—a leather-bound journal. Then a book for Mr. S.

Opal shot a look at Matthias and he gave a little shrug, his mouth curving up. "At least he'll have enough to read for a while."

Then nothing was left but for her to open her own gift from Matthias. Everyone watched as she peeled back the cloth. Inside was another layer of cloth, this one folded carefully into a small square. She could feel something hard inside it.

She shot a glance at the expectant faces around her, careful not to linger on Matthias's. As she opened the last of the wrapping, she discovered a wooden cross rested inside, shaped exactly like the metal pendant Matthias wore that had been passed down through centuries of Björk men.

This ornament wasn't strung on a leather thong but on a rich blue velvet that gave the necklace an air of elegance. Yet nothing could overshadow the detailed beauty of the cross, with the scrollwork on each of the arms. The beauty of the piece was enough to bring a surge of emotion to sting her eyes.

'Twas almost a perfect match to the cross he wore. Had he carved it himself? She met his gaze, seeing her answer in the raw emotion showing there. How many talents this man possessed.

"'Tis beautiful, Matthias. Exquisite." Holding the wooden piece in her hand, she studied the detail. He must have made it from cedar wood, because the red and blonde striations added breathtaking detail to the scrollwork.

She raised her gaze to his again, trying to infuse a little bit of her heart into her words. "Thank you."

193

He nodded, his eyes looking just a little hungry. As though he'd thought of her with every brush of the carving knife.

She wanted to ask him to tie it around her neck. But the others still looked on, making her too self-conscious to make the request just now. Mrs. S. would help if she asked, but it seemed only right for Matthias to fasten it on her.

So she settled back in her seat, turning a smile on the others. "'Tis been a wonderful Christmas. Each of you has made it most special."

Doctor Howard pushed to his feet, holding his gifts to his chest. "I heartily concur. And now, I'll bid you all good night and *Fröhliche Weihnachten.*"

Opal repeated the German expression for Merry Christmas along with the others. She'd picked up more German in the past months with the Shumeisters than she'd expected. Not that she could speak it very well, but she could understand most of the phrases Mrs. S. slipped into daily life.

Mr. S. rose to his feet as well, then moved to the fire and began to bank the coals, their sign the festivities had drawn to a close. Opal stood with the others, gathering her new treasures, along with the wrapping supplies. After bidding the older couple good-night, she headed toward the stairs.

She could feel the presence of Matthias behind her as she climbed, even if she couldn't hear the steady thump of his boots. They reached the upstairs landing, and she stopped just outside his door. She'd not thought to bring a lantern up, and shadows cloaked Matthias's face.

Shuffling sounds drifted from the doctor's room across the hall as Matthias fiddled with the handle of his door. "Let me set these down."

When he stepped into his room, moonlight spilled into the hallway in a swath as wide as the door frame. Matthias reappeared in the doorway, the light behind him outlining the breadth of his shoulders as his face sank into deeper shadows. Thankfully, he moved into the hallway, turning so the light brushed one side of him.

"Thank you for my scarf." His voice was deep and a little husky.

Heat crept into her face. "'Tis not much. Hopefully it'll help keep you warmer on the trail."

His face seemed to pinch. "Yes, I'm sure it will." But he said it as though the thought was painful. Had she misspoken? Maybe he was trying to decide whether he would keep up his life as a wanderer. Could he be contemplating building a house in the area? Maybe settling down...

Her pulse ratchetted up at the thought. But 'twas probably just her own longings seeking any sign. Maybe he was actually planning to leave as soon as possible. Maybe he was eager to be back on the trail.

She summoned her courage and did her best to keep the angst out of her voice. "When will you leave for the northern territory?"

195

His expression pinched again. It seemed her second conjecture was the correct one. "I'd rather wait 'til the end of Yule, but I hate to delay another seven days." He scrubbed a hand through his hair. "I've told myself a week won't make any difference, but then I worry I'll miss the one person who might actually know where she is."

His anguish was real, that was plain from the stark honesty in his voice and the tight lines of his jaw. Her chest ached with a little of the same pain he must be feeling.

She stepped closer, resting her free hand on his chest. "Go tomorrow. Find your sister and bring her back to us."

He placed his hand over hers, holding her there. His throat worked, but he didn't speak. Was he still not sure?

"Are you...?" He paused. His throat worked again, the sound of his breathing touching the silence. "Would you...?" He stopped again.

If he didn't finish his sentence, her heart might just burst through her chest.

But then, before she could realize his intent, he lowered his head and pressed his lips to hers, his mouth sweeping like a hawk for its prey. His kiss spoke of hunger. Need. A bit of desperation.

She tried to infuse a calm steadiness in her response. *I'll be here when you come back to me.* If a kiss could speak, that's what she wanted him to hear.

At last, he seemed to calm, and his actions turned sweet. Achingly sweet, and she almost lost her resolve to send him north. This man had her heart, she could no longer deny the fact.

He pulled away, hovering with the thinnest sliver of air between them as he seemed to struggle for breath. And she was doing the same.

Then he rested his forehead on hers, bringing his hand from her shoulder up to finger a lock of hair that had escaped her chignon. "I'll leave so I can come back again. Wait for me?"

Did he have to ask? She nodded, moving both their heads as his forehead still rested against hers. His mouth curved.

Now might be her last chance to ask him. "Matthias?"

"Hmm?"

"Will you fasten my cross?"

He lifted his head and studied her for a moment. Did he feel the same way about the significance of the act as she did? Probably not. She was turning into a sentimental sap, but this mountain man wouldn't harbor the same girlish whims.

He nodded and held out his hand. She placed the cross and ribbon in his palm, her fingers brushing against his work-worn skin.

Then she turned and tilted her chin down to give him access to her neck. She'd worn her hair up, so at least he wouldn't have to struggle with it.

His fingers grazed her collar as he worked. When he brushed her skin, a tingle swept down her back. "My fingers are too big and clumsy. There."

197

He inched back, and she turned to face him again, reaching up to finger the smooth wood and the grooves of the decoration. "The detail in your carving is remarkable. I didn't know you had that particular talent."

The lines of his face pulled into a smile, illuminated by the moonlight from his room. He reached up to brush her cheek. "Good night, Opal. Merry Christmas."

"Merry Christmas."

He stepped back and into his room. With the shadows hiding his face, they made it impossible to see if any longing marked his expression. There was no doubt the yearning in her chest proved she was already missing him. That yearning would grow much worse when he left.

Tomorrow.

Matthias guided his horse through the laden streets of the little mining town. 'Twas a jest to call the place a town really. More like a muddy hovel with more soot-covered men than any square mile should boast.

It couldn't be possible that his sister had lived here. Nor his great-aunt and great-uncle for that matter. Although the last missive he'd received had only mentioned Alanna and Uncle Enoch. Had Aunt Astrid passed on then?

Tents lined both sides of the street, and even Karl seemed reticent to slog through the mire and mass of filthy men. How in the world would he locate a particular person here? Some of the tent posts had handwritten signs affixed to them, and—wonder of wonders—one even had a telegraph wire connected to a high post, which fed down into the tent. Likely the most stable part of the whole flimsy place.

He headed that direction.

The black man inside appeared cleaner and more civilized than three-quarters of the throng outside the tent walls. "Yessuh." He sat behind a wooden trestle table that looked like it might double as a plank to feed a hungry horde of men. "I knew Mistuh Björk. Nice fella, that. Too bad about his niece."

Too bad. Matthias's hand went to his gun belt, although 'twas instinct only. He certainly didn't plan to use it on this man. Unless he'd hurt Alanna. "What about the niece?"

The man's dark brows sank low over his eyes. "She got awful sick. That's why they left."

"What kind of sick? Do you know where they went?" So many other questions clogged his mind. What kind of woman had Alanna grown into? Was she still kind and beautiful like his eight-year-old mind remembered her? Or had she weathered into a hard, careworn hag, far older than the twenty-eight years she would be now. Or...heaven-forbid... *God, please don't let her have been forced to compromise herself. Or worse, had it forced upon her in this vice-ridden place.*

The other man shrugged and glanced down at the papers on the table. "Don't know where they went. She had the consumption, or somethin' like it. Coughed a lot. Mistuh Björk was takin' her some'ere she could get better."

199

"Was that farther south? Or maybe to the west?" He gripped his coat to keep from grabbing the man and extracting the answer from him. 'Twas like living a dream to think he was actually talking to someone who'd known Alanna.

The man looked up, past Matthias. Staring, as though into the past. "Seems like he said somethin' about goin' north. Maybe some hot springs? I might be rememberin' wrong." The man focused back on Matthias, sharing an apologetic smile. "I'm sorry I can't help more."

Matthias let out a long breath. "I appreciate everything you've been able to tell me. One more question. The man's wife wasn't with them, was she? A Mrs. Astrid Björk?"

The other fellow shook his head. "No, but Mistuh Björk did mention his dear departed wife once, if memory serves."

A lump clogged Matthias's throat and he rubbed the back of his neck. He'd fought so much bitterness through the years toward his great-aunt and uncle for taking Alanna and leaving him with a family already overstuffed with eleven of their own children. Yet Enoch and Astrid were still family. And now his three remaining kinfolk had just slipped down to two.

"I'm sorry about that, Mistuh. Was she your ma?"

Matthias looked up at the man, seeing the empathy there. "My great-aunt. The lady with them is my sister."

The black man nodded, lips pinching a bit. "If I think of anythin' else, I'll be sure an' let you know. You got a place to stay?"

He shook his head. "Was planning to camp outside of town."

"That might be best, but if you decide you want a roof over yer head, Curly's is the only decent place around. You'd be layin' yer bedroll twixt two other fellas, but at least there's a heater. An' Curly makes flapjacks in the mornin's."

"I'll keep it in mind." Matthias extended his hand. "I appreciate everything."

The other man gripped his hand with a massive paw. "Glad to help."

Chapter Nineteen

Dearest Opal,

I'm sorry I've been such a tardy correspondence partner. This little angel consumes so much of my energy. By the time she's finally asleep and the most necessary chores finished, I can scarce hold my eyes open. Ezra has been more help than I can say, yet even he grows weary at times. And of course, Mara comes with food and never leaves without accomplishing more in one hour than I've managed all day. She has not one, but two little ones. I confess to succumbing to the sin of envy in more than one weak moment.

But enough of my weariness woes. I truly have nothing to complain about, as God has gifted us with the most precious babe I've ever seen. She's starting to smile, Cousin, and it lights up her face so that I can scarcely breathe for the love overwhelming my chest. I pray one day you'll meet the man God has for you, and you'll experience the kind of life-altering joy that comes when we're in His will.

Please, write soon and tell me how you spent Christmas. We feasted with Mara and Josiah and their two little ones, although Katie can hardly be called little any longer. She's almost a mother to her baby brother.

I must say farewell now, as Ruby begins to wake from her nap. All my love, dear cousin. Come see us again soon.

Yours, etc.

Tori

Sitting on the stoop of the boardinghouse's back door, Opal looked up from her letter as Charmer nuzzled her face. "Hey, boy." She pulled his head into the crook of her neck and soaked in the soft warmth of his affection. A simple letter from Tori shouldn't make her feel so homesick. Not when she was truly happy here in her new home. A place where she was needed. Depended upon, even.

She'd rather be here than the third wheel in Tori's new family. Or, fourth wheel, as it were.

Yet still, the burn of tears stung her eyes, smarting even more as a wind whipped through the little clearing, blowing against her lashes. She ducked lower to hide her face in Charmer's coat. If Matthias were here, all the light would be back in her life.

Yet that wasn't exactly true. No matter how happy he made her, he couldn't be the source of her joy. What had she read that morning? *Thou wilt shew me the path of life: in Thy*

203

presence is fullness of joy; at Thy right hand there are pleasures for evermore.

Fullness of joy. The idea fed a longing deep in her chest. God had to be the source of her joy. She was understanding that more with each passing week. *Lord, is it too much to ask for Matthias to be part of that picture?*

She could imagine them in a little house outside of town. Maybe even a bit farther into the mountains, where no sign of man's interruption had marred the landscape. Where deer and squirrels and mountain goats wandered by their cabin. Yet, close enough she could come help Mrs. S. with the baking.

Would Matthias still allow her to help? Surely, he would. He loved the couple as much as she did.

He would need to settle things with Mr. Lefton if he were going to be a permanent fixture in Mountain Bluff. Whatever the livery owner had against Matthias, surely they could resolve the matter.

She straightened and ruffled Charmer's golden head. As the Scripture said, with God showing them the path of life, they could work through anything, couldn't they?

The thrill of speed pulsed through Matthias as he leaned low over Karl's neck, the wind whipping the coarse white mane against his face. He reined the gelding around a boulder, then wove through the scattered pine and spruce trees. The creek ahead would appear quickly once he rounded that cluster of cedars.

The horse dodged right to skirt the evergreens, his muscles bunching as he anticipated the coming leap over the water. As the trees cleared, the narrow chasm loomed ahead. Matthias couldn't help the way his pulse raced as he scanned the edge of the bank for a flash of golden hair.

Opal had done more that first day than just send him sailing into the frigid water. She'd started a spark inside him that grew into a blaze he now seemed unable to fight.

That was the only reason he could account for the fact that he was, even now, pointed toward Mountain Bluff.

Karl soared over the gap between the banks, landing smoothly on the other side. After loping a few more strides, Matthias sat back in the saddle and slowed the gelding to a walk. He needed to cool his muscles for a few minutes since the evening air around them seemed to be cooling so quickly.

Hopefully he wasn't obliterating his efforts to find Alanna by going south now instead of north. He'd found one other person in that entire mining town who remembered Enoch Björk, and that man had also remembered him mentioning a hot springs farther north.

So, he'd sent wires and letters northward. As far as he'd been able to determine by the maps in the surveyor's tent, there were several areas of hot springs, especially farther north into Canada.

He could only hope his messages might find fertile ground. It would be a miracle, really, if his missives reached someone who knew Uncle Enoch or Alanna. But he'd been praying for just that.

He'd probably have to go north, but he had to see Opal one last time before he left for so many months. Or mayhap, if the Lord shone upon him, he could talk Opal into marrying him and making the trip, too. What a thrilling life that would be. Spending days riding through the wild beauty of the northern mountains, living as one with God's creation. Then nights with her snuggled under his bearskin, dreaming of the rest of their lives together.

No, he couldn't imagine any life sweeter than those images.

Hopefully, Opal would feel the same way.

Opal pulled the three pans of bread from the oven, the yeasty sourdough smell filling the air. No scent on earth could soothe a person like that of bread fresh from the oven.

The sound of voices drifted from the other room as she loosened the sides of the bread from the first pan. Mrs. S., for sure. And that male voice had a higher tone to it, like Mr. Chancellor. And there was another, a bit deeper. Her heart leapt at the thought that it could be Matthias, but she suppressed the idea.

She'd been doing a lot of that lately—imagining his voice in the other room, or seeing his profile at the end of the street or stepping from the shadows. Each time, her conjuring hopes were dashed.

She slipped the first loaf out of its pan, setting it on the rack to cool. As she moved on, the next one slid easily out. Another perfect loaf. She'd always loved being in the kitchen, yet with her father's servants bustling around that room in Riverdale, she'd never really had a chance to develop her abilities until she and Tori had come west.

Large hands gripped her waist, and she squealed as something solid pressed on her shoulder. Spinning around, she raised an elbow to fend off her attacker. But Matthias's whiskered face smiled down at her, sending her pulse racing for a far different reason.

"You're back." She pressed her hands to his chest as his settled on her sides. His green eyes seemed to drink her in, that roguish mouth tipping in a delicious smile.

"I told you I'd come back. You didn't believe me?"

She fingered the edges of his fur coat. He'd not even taken time to remove it apparently, although the buttons had been released. "I didn't think you could accomplish your mission so quickly." She studied his eyes again. "Did you learn anything?"

A bit of the smile left his face, and his hands tightened on her waist. "She'd been there. I found two people who knew them. Apparently, Alanna took ill, and my uncle decided they should go farther north in search of healing springs."

Worry pulsed in her chest, intensified by the lines that deepened under his eyes. "What kind of illness. Is it bad?"

He let out a steady stream of breath. "I don't know. I hope not."

She wanted to step into his arms, wrap him in a hug that could help ease his fears. This sister he'd not seen in almost a score of years, and he was probably wondering now how grave the sickness was. Could there be a chance he wouldn't find her before she passed away?

The thought struck so hard, it seemed to propel her toward him. She stepped into his chest, slipping her arms around the solid slab of his sides. Doing her best to infuse all the love and encouragement she could into the embrace.

He pulled her closer, pressing her to him. Clinging, almost. She sank in, letting her eyes drift shut as she inhaled the thick musky scent of man and nature that was his alone. This man held her heart. And the most remarkable part was that realizing that fact didn't scare her. Instead, it infused her with a strength and determination that made all her senses come alive.

With Matthias beside her, she could face anything. Maybe even be the strength he might need in the coming days.

"I've missed you." His gravelly voice ruffled her hair, sending a skitter down her arms.

"And I you."

The sound of the door opening made her pull back, more reluctantly than was proper.

Mrs. S. bustled in, giving them a single glance before reaching for a tin on the shelf above the work counter. "You will drink tea with us, Matthias. Ja?"

He straightened. "I need to check the postal office first. Get that mail Chancellor said was waiting."

Mrs. S. flapped her hand toward Opal. "You go, too. Get ze bundle of notions Hattie made for us."

Opal reached to loosen her apron strings, not quite able to bring herself to protest. "All right."

Walking down the street on Matthias's arm felt a bit like the fulfillment of some of her dreams, and she soaked in every word he spoke of the happenings on his trip. His description of the mining town made her thankful, once again, for this little haven in Mountain Bluff.

They stepped into the mercantile, the bell jingling over the doorway. Hattie Chancelor's head bobbed above the back counter. "Miss Boyd. Mr. Björk." Her smile lingered on Matthias as her brow scrunched. "I know what you've come for." Then she bent down to peer at something under the counter. "Here we go. For someone who doesn't come around very often, you do keep our telegraph and mail service busy."

She handed a paper across the counter, and Matthias took it. The white note seemed so flimsy in his tanned, competent hand, but Opal couldn't help but notice the way his fingers went pale where he gripped the missive.

"What can I do for you, Miss Boyd?"

Opal couldn't quite pull her gaze away from Matthias as he unfolded the telegram. "I'm, um, here to pick up a package for Mrs. Shumeister."

Matthias seemed to move in half-time, as though he dreaded the words he would find inside.

Mrs. Chancellor prattled on, but her comments didn't penetrate the quiet that settled over Opal and Matthias.

He scanned the words on the paper, and it took all her resistance not to lean over his arm to read along with him.

When he looked up, his eyes swam in so much emotion, their green seemed to darken to the color of rich pine needles. Yet 'twas impossible to tell if he were pleased or afraid.

He held the paper to her, and she took it, searching his face once more for some clue about its contents. At last, she turned her focus to the words scrawled in looping script. It took a moment to find order in them.

Brother. I have heard you are seeking me. I am thrilled to find you and hope this reaches you well. We are settled near Hot Springs Camp in the country of Canada, a place with many healing powers. Come to us if you can. We are three weeks' ride north of the Montana Territory. The town is known by all in the area. I long to see you. Alanna.

The name punctuating the final sentence seemed to leap out from the page. *His sister.* She was alive. And wanted

210

Matthias to come to her. If her health were so fragile, she wouldn't be able to travel south to them. How long would Matthias be gone?

So much swirled in her mind, she barely felt his hand at her back, turning her. She accepted the wrapped bundle from Mrs. Chancellor, then followed at Matthias's side as they left the building.

Quiet seeped over them as they followed the street back toward the boardinghouse. She should speak. Share in the joy he must be feeling after receiving news that his quest had almost been accomplished. One more journey, and he'd be reunited with his sister.

But then what?

The question slipped through her mind on a steady loop, stilling her tongue from anything she might have forced herself to speak.

And Matthias kept quiet, too.

The one time she braved a glance at him, his forehead puckered in grooves as though he were formulating an answer to a monumental problem.

But that wasn't the way it should be. Finding his lost sister should be the happiest day of his life. She couldn't allow her own fears to temper his joy.

Reaching for his arm, she infused happiness into her voice. "The news is wonderful, Matthias. You've finally received word from Alanna."

He met her gaze for a quick moment, a smile flitting over his face before it returned to the former contemplating look. "It is good news, isn't it? Great news."

She let the silence fall as they passed the two remaining buildings before the boardinghouse. Inside, they peeled off coats, and Matthias took hers to hang them both on the hooks.

"I'm going to go clean up a bit." He didn't meet her gaze, and his voice sounded weary. But then, why shouldn't it? He'd just returned from a long journey and hadn't even stopped to sit down and eat a bite.

"Dinner will be ready in a half hour or so."

He offered her a half-smile. "All right." Then he turned and walked toward the stairs.

And as she watched him trudge upward, she couldn't help but see her dreams slipping away with each retreating step.

Chapter Twenty

atthias sank on the bed and dropped his face into his hands. Alanna. He'd finally found her. But what was he to do about it now? He'd known things were different the moment he stepped into the kitchen earlier and saw Opal working at the counter. The sight of her there was like coming home. He belonged with this woman, and every part of him knew it.

And every part of him loved that fact, all the way until he'd read Alanna's words about the healing springs in Canada. Healing was what she needed, but the primitive mountain country in Canada was the last thing Opal needed. She craved protection. Wanted to be secreted away in a safe little hamlet. Just going with him for a ride through the mountains was enough excitement for her. The reminder of their race on the way back from her cousin's home made his mouth pull into a bit of grin.

But it faded quickly. He couldn't drag Opal through the months of mountain travel to reach Canada, then settle her in a primitive country where they probably didn't even have access to mail service. There was no telling how far Alanna had been forced to travel to send him word.

Yet he had to go to his sister. He'd sworn to himself over and over that if he ever found Alanna, he'd never let them be separated by distance again. He'd always keep family near.

God, what would you have me do? He raised his face upward, his gaze seeking out the grain in the wooden ceiling. *Should I go to Alanna or stay with Opal?* No answer boomed in a voice of thunder. No heavenly hand appeared to write a response on the wooden beams.

Sinking back against the soft cotton of the quilt, he lay on his back and let his mind ponder. He had to go to Alanna. There was really no question there. She was his sister. His blood relative. And if she was sick, she would need someone to look after her. Old Uncle Enoch wouldn't be able to accomplish the job suitably. The aged man probably needed looking after himself.

So…his only other option with Opal was to ask her to go with him. If she'd agree, they could be married here in Mountain Bluff, then head northward. This journey was sure to be quite a wedding trip.

Opal balanced a platter in each hand as she pushed the door open with her hip. The stewed meat smelled perfectly

214

scrumptious, yet her stomach had churned itself into a tight knot.

"Let me have those."

She jumped at the voice, then eased out a breath as she looked over at Matthias.

He was striding toward her with purpose marking the set of his shoulders. She allowed him to take one of the platters, then carried the other to the table herself. "Mrs. S. just went to call everyone for dinner."

"I know. And I told her you and I would be taking our meal out of doors. How soon can you be ready?"

She paused and looked at him. Maybe his expression would give a hint as to what in the land of the saints he was talking about.

His face held a self-assured grin.

"Ready for what?"

"We're going for a ride."

"In the cold?" She shot a glance toward the window. The light outside was turning a dusky hue, which meant the temperature would be dropping quickly, too. Not that she should argue against time alone with Matthias.

She turned back to him. "Would you rather we eat in the kitchen?" Or maybe he wanted a quiet place to kiss her. Her pulsed kicked up just thinking about it.

And from the way one corner of his mouth tipped higher than the other, he could read her thoughts.

Perhaps she should go along with what he asked. Although, she'd not go forward blindly. She didn't

215

completely trust her self-control when she was in this man's arms.

"I should check with Mrs. S. to see if 'tis all right if we're not present for the meal."

He moved toward her. "I already did. She said she'll be glad to be rid of us." Taking her shoulders, he turned her toward the stairs. "Go do whatever you need to be ready. I'll pack some food."

She followed his nudge toward the stairs. The meal was set for the Shumeisters to sit down and eat, and she'd need to add some extra woolen layers under her skirt if they were going to ride as the sun dipped behind the horizon.

In a matter of minutes, Matthias was sitting bareback atop his gelding. In his buckskin breeches and sitting astride, he looked like one of the Roman gods she remembered from the paintings that had lined the library walls at Riverdale. Possessing a strength one could only imagine.

"Grip my arm and I'll pull you up."

She obeyed his directive, and the effort to lift her seemed to barely faze him. As though she weighed nothing more than his saddle pack.

She settled her skirts to cover her legs and scooted a little to put a respectable distance between them. Yet with the slope of Karl's back, 'twas hard not to slide back down against Matthias.

"Ready?"

"When you are."

The horse jolted as he started forward, and she scrambled to grab Matthias's side to keep herself from falling backward.

He chuckled and took one of her hands, then placed it so she hugged his body. "'Tis all right to hold on."

She did the same with her other and tried to relax into the rhythm of Karl's stride.

As the trail climbed, the shadows of dusk lengthened, casting an almost surreal pall over the landscape.

"Where are we going?" She straightened to see the trail over Matthias's broad shoulder.

"Almost there." Although something in his tone made her think he wished their destination were much farther. Maybe all the way north to Canada.

At least his deep contemplation from earlier had given way to his usual good humor.

When they reached a little open area, he reined in the gelding beside a large rock. "Here's a good spot." That rock would provide a nice table.

She slid from the horse's back, and he did the same, then she opened the satchel he'd prepared and laid out the food. They'd need to eat with their hands it seemed, as he'd not packed any forks, but the company would be worth any minor inconvenience.

After he spoke a simple prayer to bless the food, they started into the meal. A silence settled over them and seemed to grow thicker with each bite. She should say something, but nothing sprang to mind, save the topic of his sister and his

217

impending journey. And the thought of hearing him say he was leaving was more than she could bear just now. 'Twas hard enough getting down the tiny bites she managed to swallow.

At last, he finished his helping and wiped his hands on the cloth he'd stuffed in the pack. When he offered it to her, she took the rag and did the same.

He raised his brows at the food still left on her dish. "Not hungry?"

"Not much." She started to wrap it back up. She had a feeling he was getting ready to tell her his plans, and the last thing she wanted was for the smell of the meat to mix with her roiling nerves and resurrect what little she'd eaten.

He waited until she'd repacked their entire food bundle. There was nothing left for her to do now without making her avoidance obvious. She forced herself to meet his gaze with as convincing a smile as she could muster. "You're going to Canada, aren't you?"

His eyes grew fathomless, the green in them so deep, if she sank into them she would never resurface. "I need to." He paused long enough for the silence to tighten in her middle. "Which means I have a question for you."

Taking her hand in his, he threaded her fingers through his own. "I'd like you to go with me. I'd like you to marry me. Will you?" He never took those piercing eyes from hers, locking her tight within their depths.

She struggled to draw in breath. Worked hard to focus on his words. On the deeper meaning of all he was asking. "Marry you?"

That was what she'd wanted. But to move north? Into the wilderness. She dropped her gaze to their joined hands, focusing on the way their fingers wove together in an easy pattern. Could she go to a place completely unknown? Not even in the same country. How could she go so far from Tori and little Ruby? And the Shumeisters. How could she leave this life she'd come to love? This safety.

"I know it would be hard," he said. "But no matter what we face, I'd keep you safe, I promise. And I'll build you a good home. I'll make you happy. You have my troth."

His words seemed to die away, and she kept her focus on their joined fingers. She loved this man more than she'd ever thought possible. Could she give up everything else in her life she loved, just to be his wife?

"If you need time to think about it, I understand. I should leave within the next few days, but take until then if you need it." He paused, and she could hear his long exhale. "I know I'm asking a lot, Opal. But I love you. I can't imagine leaving without asking—praying—you'll marry me."

She did look up at him then. Saw the raw emotion raging in his eyes. Felt the burn stinging her own. "I know you need to find your sister, Matthias. But I don't think I can go with you. I don't think I can leave my own family, these people. I'm sorry."

She looked away, fighting to hold back the surge of tears. She wouldn't be able to restrain them long, though. Gripping the satchel with the remnants of their meal, she stood and headed toward the horse. "We should go back now. 'Tis almost dark."

Matthias left. Less than twelve hours after she'd said she wouldn't marry him, he rode out of her life forever.

Opal forced the knife through the thick potato. She shouldn't be surprised he'd departed so soon. After all, if his sister were very ill, every day might determine whether he saw her before the worst happened. Yet she couldn't stop the way his sudden leaving fractured her heart a little deeper. He'd not lingered in case she changed her mind.

Holding the half piece of potato over the stew pot, she diced it into smaller pieces that landed in the water with a *plunk*. Something else she couldn't stop was the question which had echoed through her all morning. *Had she made the wrong choice?* Each time the thought pulsed through her, it raised the burn tears to her eyes. How could she have let Matthias ride out of her life? Could she really just carry on as though she'd never met him? Maybe she should ride out and catch up to him. There was still time for her to purchase a horse from the livery—Butter, if Mr. Lefton would allow it— and catch up with Matthias. Yet, could she bring herself to leave everything that made her feel so safe? If only she could talk through this with someone.

Mrs. S. bustled through the kitchen door, a wooden crate in her arms. "Zis should carry us through another week." She plopped the crate on the table with a *thunk*, then propped her fists on her ample hips and turned to survey the room.

Opal spun back to the potatoes she was slicing. Her eyes were probably red-rimmed, which the older woman would spot immediately. Even though part of her wanted someone to confide in, she wouldn't be able to get through the whole dilemma without tears taking over.

The swish of skirts behind her gave the barest warning before warm, strong hands rested on her shoulders, turning her around. Opal let them pull her, reluctantly meeting Mrs. S.'s searching gaze. Except she couldn't quite meet those all-seeing eyes, so she focused on the cleft of her chin.

"Liebling. What is it?"

The gentle concern in her tone was more than Opal's defenses could withstand. She gathered a fortifying breath and told Mrs. S. about declining Matthias's proposal.

The older woman listened, her thin lips pressed together and her eyes taking every nuance of Opal's story. "And you are sad about your choice?"

Opal nodded. "I wanted to say yes. But I don't want to leave here. I'm happy with you and Mr. S. And I love the baking."

221

Mrs. S. waved the comments away. "Posh. Ve are two old people. You must not zink of us when you decide about ze rest of your life. Tell me now...what does your Heavenly Father say?"

She nibbled the edge of her lip. "I'm not sure. I've asked Him, of course. But He's not made my answer clear. I feel like it would be foolish to choose a man over my family and friends." She motioned around the room. "And this wonderful life He's given me. How could I leave it?" After meeting Mrs. S.'s gaze again, she wrapped her arms around her waist. "Even for Matthias." Yet, why did she feel like she was trying to convince herself? The very thought of leaving this place was preposterous.

"Do you love ze man?" Mrs. S. backed away and held her with those sharp eyes.

"I think so, but it doesn't—"

"What keeps you from marrying him zen?"

She glared at the woman. Had Mrs. S not heard a word she'd said? "He's left for Canada. If I married him, I'd be leaving everything I know and love, all my family and friends."

Mrs. S. still gripped Opal's shoulders, but she slid her hold down to unwrap Opal's arms, taking each hand in her own. "When Gunther and I were first married, we lived in a little village north of Dresden. We had a nice life there, starting our bakery and enjoying all our neighbors. I thought we would be happy there always."

Opal sank back against the counter behind her, settling into the chance to divert her weary thoughts.

"But zen Gunther's brother sent us a letter from America, telling us all ze wonderful stories of zis place. He would read ze letter to me each night, and we would imagine new parts to his stories. To me, it was a game we shared. But zen one evening, Gunther took my hands and said he thought God was calling us to go to America. First, I thought he was telling a joke. Zen I was afraid. How could God want me to leave my happy life?"

Her eyes glazed as she seemed to sink into the memories, and Opal couldn't help the overwhelming love for this woman that washed through her chest. Her life had been similar to Opal's in some ways, except she'd already been married to Mr. Shumeister at the time of their move. She'd already promised her life to him, to follow wherever he felt God leading them.

But Opal had been ready to marry Matthias before the telegraph from his sister. She'd wanted to commit her life in that same way. Yet, had she known what it would cost her…

"My Gunther was patient with me, but he felt God's calling so strongly. I thought he'd gone cuckoo."

Opal couldn't help but return the woman's soft smile.

"But zen God reminded me of ze Scripture where He says there is a time for everything under ze sun. I knew zat my time in Germany was done. When I told Gunther we could follow his dream, such happiness came over him, I knew I had been wrong to withhold it. God had us in His

223

hand. He put us together. He gave ze dream of America to my husband. And He would give us blessings in ze new land."

Mrs. S. squeezed her hands. "And you, my Opal, are one of ze blessings he has given us. But I am reminded again zat He has a time for planting, and a time for plucking up. If He has called you to be plucked, He will take care of you wherever He plants you again."

She raised her hand to rest on Opal's cheek. The warmth of her work-roughened palm seeped in like a comforting blanket. "You will always have our love, no matter here or in Canada. But if your heart is with ze man who rode away zis morning, you'd best get your horse and go after him."

A time to be plucked. Somehow the idea didn't sound quite so terrifying as it had that morning—or the night before.

Chapter Twenty-One

atthias nudged Karl up the steady incline of the deer trail as it wrapped around the side of the mountain. Maybe he shouldn't press the horse so hard, but they had so much land to travel between here and Canada.

And there was nothing holding him back any longer.

He'd said his goodbyes to Mutti and Vatti, promising to write. Shook the doctor's hand in farewell. Even looked into Opal's beautiful, red-rimmed blue eyes and told her he wished her well.

Then he'd mounted Karl and not looked back. Until he was almost out of sight anyway, but Opal hadn't been there watching him. Apparently, she didn't feel the same love that raged in his own chest, twisting like a knife point deeper and deeper.

Perhaps he should buy another horse at the next town. That way he could alternate riding the two mounts and cover ground faster. The sooner he reached Canada, the sooner he'd see his sister again. And the sooner he could leave the pain of Opal's rejection behind.

225

Although it might take more than distance to escape her memory.

"You are sure you have everyzing you need? I will give you another bag."

Opal tugged her carpet bag closed and fastened the buckle, then turned to Mrs. S. "There won't be room on the poor horse for me to sit. Besides, I have everything. I won't be needing these ruffled gowns in Canada anyway." Only one more practical woolen skirt and shirtwaist, like those she already wore. A change of underthings, several blankets, and food. Lots of food. Hopefully, she could catch up with Matthias before nightfall, because she didn't have a bearskin to snuggle under this time.

"Use my wages to send this trunk to Tori when you find someone going that direction with a wagon. I've put a letter just inside the lid." Opal finally stopped to study the older woman, who had her skirt gripped in both hands, wringing it as though fighting the urge to do something to stop this madness.

Stepping closer, Opal wrapped her hands around Mrs. S.'s arms. "I'll be all right. I promise. God will take care of us, you'll see. And I'll have Charmer to protect me, too."

Mrs. S. nodded, although her pinched lips bespoke a myriad of emotions that weren't so agreeable.

226

Opal chuckled and pulled the older woman into a hug. "You're the one who talked me into this. And now you're disregarding all your own advice."

"I should be placed in ze stocks for encouraging you to go." She returned the hug with a strength that never seemed to match her short, round physique.

Pulling back, Opal looked into those sweet, brown eyes. "Now that I finally faced my fear, I know this is what I need to do. I love Matthias, and I know God brought him for me. Now I need to go where he is. To be by his side and help him follow his dreams." Opal nodded, trying her best to let her face show the certainty that had taken root in her chest. "This is right. I feel it."

Mrs. S. nodded, patting Opal's arm. "I know. But I will still miss you."

And, of course, that brought on the tears again. Opal wrapped the woman in another hug as hot, salty drops leaked down her face. She'd never been loved by anyone except Tori, not really. Now she had these two wonderful people that God had placed in her life for a season.

And hopefully, she also had Matthias's love, if he could forgive her for refusing him. She was pretty sure he understood her fear. She wouldn't be setting out on her own into the mountain wilderness if she didn't feel strongly he'd welcome her.

At last, she finished her goodbyes to the Shumeisters and Doctor Howard. Thankfully, the doctor had come back to the boardinghouse for lunch, so she'd not had to track him down for a farewell. Mr. and Mrs. S. had wanted to accompany her to the livery and see her off, but she convinced them not to. She'd already shed enough tears in this farewell.

Now, 'twas time to purchase a horse and be off. Lord willing, Matthias had traveled the same trail he'd taken her on to see the geyser, and she'd be able to find his horse's tracks. *Please take me to him quickly, Lord.*

The sound of metal pounding echoed through the street as she neared the livery with Charmer at her heels. As she expected, Mr. Lefton was working at his anvil in the little area to the left of the doorway. He stopped when he caught sight of her and straightened, wiping a rag across his brow.

He gave her a calculating look, as though he were debating whether to welcome her in or raise his mallet to run her off. This was the same indecision she'd sensed the other times she'd met him since that day of the run-in when they were decorating the Christmas tree.

She raised her chin and gave him a formal smile. "Hello, Mr. Lefton. I've come to ask if Butter is for sale."

He raised his brows at her. "Renting him's not good enough for ya, anymore?"

"I'm leaving town and need a mount. I'd like to purchase him if possible. Otherwise, do you have another reliable horse?" A spurt of angst tried to rise at the thought of setting out on a horse she didn't know. But surely, no matter how much this man hated Matthias, he wouldn't sell her a horse likely to injure her.

"Goin' to visit your cousin again?" His tone was almost jeering, which raised her defenses.

"No, sir. I'm moving northward."

Now he looked more interested than she'd have expected. "North, you say? Found a job or gettin' hitched?"

She narrowed her gaze. It really wasn't this man's concern where she was going and why. And she didn't plan to be the source of Mountain Bluff gossip in coming months either. "Did you decide whether I can purchase Butter?"

He wiped his hands on the same rag he'd used on his face, then tossed it over the anvil and sauntered toward the barn's hallway. "Well, now. I'm not sure." His tone had gone as leisurely as his stride. "If you're goin' to the goldfields to flaunt your wiles, I'm not sure as I'd want old Butter to get caught up in that."

She let out a huff. He was trying to rile her, and with a comment like that, he was doing a pretty good job. "Mr. Lefton, you know far better than to think I'd do something so disreputable. I won't taint your horse, I can promise you."

He paused at one of the stalls and turned to her, leaning back against the post. "In that case, maybe you're plannin' to run off an' marry a farmer. I can't be sendin' Butter to a life of pullin' plows and such."

If she weren't a lady, she would slug the man here and now. Instead, she gritted her teeth. "Will you sell him to me or not?"

He leveled his gaze at her. "You tell me where you're goin', and I'll let you take that horse you love so much. You refuse to say, and you may as well get walkin'."

Charmer growled low in his throat. She reached down to rest a hand on his head, memories flashing of when he'd attacked Gultcher. Thankfully, the dog still stood by her side this time. But it felt good to know she had an ally.

She returned her focus to the stubborn livery owner. "Mr. Lefton, why is it any concern of yours where I'm going?"

He crossed his arms. "You're taking my horse. It's my business."

If only she could grip his shoulders and shake some sense into the man. "If I buy him, he'll be *my* horse."

He just stood there, propped against the stall, arms barricaded across his chest, and the most belligerent look on his face she'd ever seen.

Finally, she let out a huff loud enough to show her frustration. "Canada. I'm going to Canada where I'm to be married." Although hopefully they'd find a town with a sheriff or minister who could marry them long before they reached Canada. Not only would it be improper to travel for days alone with Matthias, but her self-restraint could only be tested so far. Even she knew that.

"Marryin' that Indian lover, are ya?" The way he growled the words raised her ire even higher.

"Mr. Lefton, my horse, if you please."

After another glare, the man finally straightened and turned back down the hall. "Ten dollars for the horse and saddle. I'll have him ready straightaway."

As the man faded into the dim hallway, Opal let out a long breath. Finally. A few more minutes and she'd be on her way to Matthias. If she left now and rode through the night, she should catch up with him by morning.

The trail looked similar to the way it had when Opal had traveled this route with Matthias. Yet with most of the snow melted, the landscape certainly looked more barren. It required her full focus to stay on the path they'd taken before. Every few strides, she'd see a hoof print that must be from Matthias's horse.

She pushed Butter as fast as she dared, yet she couldn't afford to lose the trail or miss the tracks if Matthias had departed it.

Lord, let him camp early for the night. That might be the only way she could catch up. It would be much slower going once darkness set in, yet she had to keep moving. If she lost the trail or let him get too far ahead, she'd never find him.

And that thought scared her more than anything.

She hadn't really let herself consider what would happen if she couldn't locate Matthias. After all, if this was the Lord's plan, He would guide her, right? *Show me, Lord.*

One section at a time. That's all she had to travel. Little by little, she could close the distance between them.

The rest of the day progressed slowly, with the terrain ranging from rocky mountain side to valleys covered in winter grass and mud. The mud was the best blessing of all, because it showed clearly the big white gelding's hoof prints, which allowed her to move faster.

As dusk began to fall, she stopped at the edge of a cluster of trees to relieve herself and pull food from her pack. Charmer plopped down as though the day's travel had stolen all his strength. Butter tore into the clusters of crunchy grass, making her wish she could linger for a while and let him eat dinner, too.

"Sorry, boy." She patted his neck as she pulled up on the reins and prepared to mount. "We need to make time while there's still light."

"We sure do."

Opal spun, caught sight of a horse, and lifted her gaze to face the man she'd thought to never see again. "Mr. Lefton. What are you doing here?"

The livery owner's expression was that of a pug faced dog, intent on protecting a slab of meat from all intruders. "Came to finally see that Indian lover get a taste of what he dishes out."

Had the man gone completely mad? She'd wondered if his strange grudge against Matthias could be the effect of an unsteady mind. And maybe now he'd finally tipped fully off the wagon.

She kept her voice even and genial. "Mr. Lefton, I'm not sure what you think Matthias has done, but he's really a good man. And besides, you don't need to worry about his presence any longer. We're going north and most likely won't be back. You can return to town and lay your angst to rest."

"You're right." His eyes narrowed, and his voice dipped with an edge of steel. Actions that didn't match his agreeable words.

Charmer growled low in his throat, more menacing than his warning earlier that day. The dog didn't like this man anymore than she did.

Still, she forced an air of relief. "Good. I'm sorry you've come all this way, but I hope you have a pleasant ride back to town."

He shifted in his saddle, and she caught a glimpse of something in his lap. The long, metal barrel of his rifle.

She couldn't quite take her eyes off the weapon as he raised it higher, aiming it directly at her. The world seemed to slow around her, as though this were all a nightmare. Surely any minute she would wake up, pulse racing.

The man nudged his horse forward, stopping just a few feet in front of her. Close enough that she could see the red splotches on his cheeks and the wiry brown strands of his beard. An unusual smell crept to her. Something like a mixture of horse and cologne water. A memory flicked through her mind, raising the hairs on her neck the same way they had the last time she smelled this scent. Had Lefton been watching her that day?

"You're right when you said I wouldn't need to worry about him stickin' around any longer. Thing is, I have a little point I need to make before we say our farewells." He kept the rifle trained on her as he slid off the horse. He performed the movement so easily, never wavering in his aim, as though he'd had plenty of practice.

She needed to do something. Say something that would stop whatever madness he had planned.

Before she could form words, Charmer lunged forward in a yellow blur, releasing a savage bark. Lefton was prepared for the attack, and met the dog with a blow from the butt of his rifle.

Charmer flew backwards with a yelp that pierced Opal's heart. He was only down for a second, though, then struggled to his feet and seemed to summon strength for another attack.

This time Lefton charged him, swinging the gun like a club.

Opal screamed. Part of her knew she should mount Butter and hightail it, but she couldn't leave Charmer to fight this monster alone. As Lefton's rifle connected with the dog again, she leapt toward him, aiming to grab the weapon from his hands. Or at least slow him down.

Lefton caught her with a strong vice-like grip around her upper arms, pinning them to her side. His other hand finally dropped the rifle, but he had such a secure hold on her, she had no way to reach for it. The ruffian's arms were as strong as Samson's from the Bible.

234

She twisted to see where Charmer had gone, but she wasn't prepared to see the lump of golden hair lying on the ground by a large rock. A sob caught in her throat. "You killed him." She fought to free herself from this ogre, but Lefton gripped tighter, his massive paws closing off the blood flow in her arms.

"Be still."

She obeyed, although every part of her screamed against it. The ache in her chest twisted so it was hard to breathe.

Lefton's rough hands moved to her wrists, jerking them upward and shooting knives of pain through her upper arms. Another rough texture tightened around her wrists, and the fear pressing on her chest sent her pulse thudding through her temples.

"Why are you doing this?" She tried to twist around to look at him, but he jerked her hands high and tugged the coarse rope tighter around her wrists.

She clamped her jaw to keep a cry of pain from escaping. *God, help me.*

"Now you're gonna get back on your horse. Then keep followin' that trail until we meet up with your man." He yanked her sideways toward Butter, and she scrambled to catch her footing.

Her right boot caught on her skirt hem, pulling her down and stealing the balance she'd almost regained. She landed hard on her right knee.

"Get up." He barked the command, then the force of a boot slammed into her thigh. Hands dragged her upward, shooting another pain through her arms and shoulders.

She cried out, leaning hard to the left as she fought to get her feet back underneath her. She had to get away from this man. This monster.

Then his solid grip landed at her waist, and she could feel the vice of it even through her coat. The next moment, her feet lifted off the ground and he hoisted her into saddle.

Butter shifted underneath her, and she did her best to loosen her legs around his sides, despite the way she wanted to cling to him. If the horse bolted with her hands tied behind her back, she'd have no way to control the animal.

"There." Lefton barely spared her a glance before grabbing her reins and pulling Butter around to follow back to his own horse. As he hefted his bulk up into the saddle, she couldn't help but stare at the sheer size of the man. All that muscle from pounding iron in the smithy. She'd have no way to overpower him with her willowy frame.

She'd have to outwit him instead.

As he settled himself and gathered his reins in one hand and hers in the other, he looked around. "Now. We keep following that same trail you were takin'. We'd best get a move on while there's still a snatch of light."

The thought that had been nursing in her chest now bloomed into fully formed certainty. "What do you want with Matthias?"

A snort issued from the man, but he didn't otherwise respond. Just kicked his horse forward, dragging hers along with him.

As she took a final look back at her sweet friend, lying still in the cold, she bit down another sob. *Thank you.*

As they rode, heavy dusk fell, making the tracks harder to find. Part of her felt almost relieved that this man who obviously intended ill for Matthias may not be able to find him. Yet that left her alone with the brute. And there was no telling what he might do in anger if his plans went awry.

Lefton seemed to know where he was going—or maybe he was just better at tracking than she was—because he moved them along at a faster clip. If they were still on the correct trail, they might actually reach Matthias sometime tonight.

As the day faded, darkness sank over the land. Yet an almost full moon lit the sky, giving enough light to their path that Lefton kept them moving. He didn't seem inclined to speak, either. The few times she'd tried to question him, he either ignored her or answered with a single grunt.

So, she resigned herself to sitting quietly, yet she sent a litany of silent prayer upward. Scraps of verses from the Psalms and Jesus's teachings sprang to her mind, giving her something to focus on as she tried to remember the rest of each passage.

Hours must have passed, and still they rode on. She should be exhausted by now. In fact, her eyes did seem eager to close, yet her muscles were as tight as the knot in her midsection.

She would need to be alert for what was to come.

Chapter Twenty-Two

The distant sky to Opal's right was just beginning to lighten when Lefton finally reined in their horses. "Shouldn't be much farther. We'll stretch our legs for a minute."

How did he know it wouldn't be much farther? But she didn't dare ask. Either he could read a lot more into the tracks than she'd imagined possible, or he had some kind of unusual instinct.

He dismounted with a groan, then came around to her. As he reached up to grip her waist, she fought the urge to lean away from him. Yet, she desperately needed to relieve herself, and making him angry just now would just work against her. She'd need to be smart about when she made her move. And if there was any way possible, she needed to warn Matthias. If he really was nearby, maybe she could sneak away and find him.

"You can go to that tree there an' do your business, but no farther. I'll have my rifle trained on you the whole time."

She glanced at the tree he motioned at, not more than fifteen feet away from them. And no other plants nearby that would help to hide her. "There's no privacy there." Her voice sounded weaker than she meant for it to, but the whole scene seemed a bit like she was looking at it through a glass window. Perhaps she was more tired than she thought.

"It's private enough."

"I need my hands untied." She twisted to show her bindings behind her back.

"Figure out a way." His jaw locked at a hard angle.

She didn't argue again, just struggled through the task. Doing her best to use her skirts and the tree trunk to protect herself from his view, she prayed that the darkness covered the remainder of her modesty.

When she stepped from around the tree, a strange smell touched her nose. Wood smoke.

She glanced at Lefton, but he still stood sentry by their horses. Had he picked up on the scent before, and that was why he thought they were near Matthias? A bead of excitement thrummed through her chest.

If she could warn him somehow, he would be able to get the better of Lefton. He could save them both. With God's help, of course. *Show me what to do, Lord.*

She stepped toward the man, but he waved the rifle at her.

"Just stay there by that tree."

She paused, not quite sure what he intended.

He approached, and in the darkness, she could barely tell the outline of a rope looped over his shoulder. As he circled around behind her, that rifle never wavered in its aim. He gripped the rope binding her wrists and jerked her backward.

That now-familiar pain shot through her upper arms, and the skin at her wrists ached from his rough handling. He pushed her against the coarse bark of the tree, and the putrid warmth of his breath touched her cheek as he wrapped a rope around her waist and the trunk.

He worked for several minutes tying her to the tree, and Opal worked to force her mind to focus on how she could escape with this new turn of events. Maybe she could spread her arms so the rope he tied would be loose enough for her to escape later.

But when he gave a jerk hard enough to squeeze all the air from her lungs, she couldn't help a gasp, nor could she hold her arms out against his strength. It seemed she'd need another option for escape.

Did he plan to leave her here while he went to search for Matthias? Maybe she could call out or find a way to warn him as soon as Lefton set off.

Matthias tossed a final log on the fire and settled back on the fallen tree he'd been using as a seat. He reached for his cup of coffee and wrapped both hands around it, staring into the leaping flames as they licked at the new wood.

Day two on the trail. The sense of adventure should have settled deep inside him by now. Instead, he couldn't shake this feeling of loss that pressed down on him. He'd given Opal the chance to come with him. Practically begged her. But she'd made her choice, and he'd had to make his own.

Now he just had to force his stubborn heart to move on.

Wind whistled through the trees, rustling the hair at his nape with its icy chill and whipping the fire into a flurry. In the distance, he could hear the mournful call as the air soared through valleys and between cliffs. He wasn't far from one of the tallest ranges in the area, and the echoes a gale made through the rocks could be almost eerie. Like a woman calling.

The sounds seemed so real this morning, he could almost distinguish the word *help*. It came in steady succession, as though a person were calling out to him.

And the wind wasn't anywhere near a gale.

He focused on the sounds. They had to be made by a human. Wind and rock couldn't be so distinct, nor so consistent, could they?

Reaching for his rifle, he pushed to his feet and turned to identify the exact direction. It seemed to be coming from the south, the way he'd traveled yesterday.

He started back down that trail, using his long stride to eat up the ground. Then the call came again, clearer than any time before. Definitely a woman screaming for help.

He could taste his pulse as he broke into a run. Was that Opal's voice? What would she be doing out here? 'Twas too much to think she might have come after him. Changed her mind. Yet his irrational heart grabbed at the idea, propelling him forward as urgency pulsed through him.

He was close now, which meant he needed to know what he might be running into. Was she caught on the edge of a cliff? Maybe her horse had thrown her, and she was lying on the ground with a broken leg.

Surging forward, he rounded the bend in the trail where it skirted a boulder on his left. Opal's last cry had been almost half a minute before, and his mind conjured images of her slipping off the edge of a precipice. Rolling down the rock-strewn hill. Smashing against boulders and pounding against sharp, bone-crushing juts in the stone.

Emerging into a small clearing, the sight before him caught him up short. At a lone tree in the center, a figure sat against the trunk.

Opal.

"Matthias." She looked as though she would run to him, yet she was held in place by ropes around her chest.

The sight clogged his mind with a momentary confusion as he tried to make sense of what exactly was going on.

"Untie me." She strained forward again. "Hurry."

A quick scan of the area revealed no one else in the clearing, so he moved forward. He pulled his knife from its sheath at his belt, then crouched beside Opal. "What are you doing here? Who did this?"

He took a second to drink in her features, those blue eyes that held enough fear to plant the same emotion in his own chest.

"'Tis Lefton. He's gone to find you. You're in danger." Her chest heaved with each declaration, as though she'd run a distance to find him.

The picture her words formed in his mind was spotted with holes but gave him enough focus to turn his knife to the rope binding her. "Did he bring you out here?"

"Followed me. I left a few hours after you, planning to catch up with you and tell you I do want to marry you. He must have followed me after I retrieved Butter from the livery. He made his presence known last night, then kept me tied while we followed your trail. I don't know what he plans, Matthias, but 'tis bad. We have to leave while he's gone to look for you."

As her words poured out in a frenzy, his mind hovered on one single fact, focusing with a clarity that sent a surge of joy through his chest. *I do want to marry you.*

He turned his full focus to her face. Her beautiful, angelic face. Placing a hand on her cheek, he drew her gaze to his. So much he wanted to say, yet one desire took over as he lowered his mouth to hers in a simple kiss. He did his best to pour every bit of his love and joy into the quick press of his mouth, then he drew back.

He could no longer ignore the other bit of news she'd spewed. "How long has Lefton been gone?" With his knife, he went back to work on the rope. If the man had tracked him through the night, it would be an easy job to follow his remaining trail during the lighter dawn hours. But why hadn't he run into Lefton on his way here?

"Probably a quarter hour, at least. I'm sure he's heard me calling to you. I was afraid he'd come back for me, but I had to warn you."

Something wasn't right here. Matthias sliced through the last of the rope and slipped his knife back in its sheath as he turned to scan the edge of the clearing. Lefton wouldn't be stupid enough to let her warn him unless he had a plan to use it to his advantage.

And that's when he saw the trees shift, saw a man step into the clearing.

Lefton held a rifle trained at them, and Matthias rose to face him, his hand going to the knife at his belt.

"Keep your hands where I can see 'em." Lefton advanced until he was a dozen feet away, close enough to make the sinister grin on his face clear.

Matthias slowly pulled his hands away from his coat, holding them out to his side. Prayed Opal stayed put. "What do you want, Lefton?"

The grin died from the man's features, fading into a scowl so fierce his cheeks and neck mottled red with his anger. "I want you to taste a piece of what you dished out on that prairie five years ago. You're gonna watch her die, screamin' and cryin' a miserable death. And there'll be nothin' you can do about it." The man took a menacing step closer, waving the gun from Matthias to Opal. "The difference is, you won't have to spend the rest of your sorry life grievin' her. I'll not let you go free, just so you can torture more innocent people."

There was a savage gleam in the man's eyes. And his comment about five years ago made no sense. He must be plain crazy, which meant he was capable of anything. And it might be impossible to guess his actions.

How could he disarm him? How could he keep Lefton's anger focused away from Opal? "Your strife is with me, Lefton. Opal has no part in it. Send her on her way, and you can torture me all you want." The words sounded crazy even as he said them, but maybe the man would agree.

That malicious grin crept back over his face. "I'll torture you all I want, don't you worry about that." He motioned with his rifle. "Toss your weapons over by those trees. Starting with your blade."

Matthias eased his hand toward his knife. Should he take the chance to aim the metal at Lefton's heart? He was pretty good aim with the weapon, but he'd have to be quick to make an accurate throw before the man shot him.

Lefton shifted the barrel toward Opal. "You make one quick move and she dies. I won't even stop to think about it."

That was a chance he wasn't willing to take. With a slow, smooth motion, he pulled back his coat and withdrew the knife, then tossed it toward the edge of the clearing.

"Now that rifle."

With that same methodical speed, he bent low to pick up the rifle where he'd laid it on the ground, then tossed it the same direction. He couldn't help a glance at Opal. Did she have any weapons?

"Now the rest of it."

Matthias pinched his mouth. Would the man search him? He'd best pull out the smaller blade tucked in the pocket of his boot. With that thrown away, he straightened and turned back to Lefton.

The man had a nervous edge to him that hadn't been there before. Was that sweat beading his brow? Matthias tensed, preparing to react to whatever blow came next.

He wasn't prepared for the crack of the rifle.

Chapter Twenty-Three

The bullet slammed into Matthias's leg, knocking it out from under him. He threw his hands out in front to break his fall, landing hard on the rocky ground.

Opal screamed, and pain shot through his wrists. Then a sharper stab struck his calf. The bullet.

He pushed up to a sitting position, then gripped his leg where it felt like flames licked at his skin. He had to force his focus back on the man holding the rifle. What would the lunatic do next?

Lefton looked a little pale, but he still had that blasted gun pointed at them. "Now lay flat on your belly." He waved the gun toward Opal. "That gal better stay put, right there against the tree."

Matthias obeyed the command, shifting around so his chest rested on the ground. The fire in his leg felt like a crimson poker iron scalding through his skin. It was easier to drag the leg than lift it, but he made sure he lay with his head close to Opal and his face turned to watch Lefton's next move.

The brute stepped forward, pulling a rope from over his shoulder. "You move, Björk, an' I'll shoot yam again."

The thought of another pain like the one scalding his leg was enough to stop him from even breathing. Yet this might be his only chance to get the jump on Lefton.

The man grunted as he reached down to grab Matthias's wrists.

Matthias flipped over, preparing to kick up at the oaf and knock him backward.

But Lefton's giant paws had such a grip on his arms, those powerful hands built up from years of pounding an anvil held him against the ground like a buffalo pinning a frog.

Then Lefton's massive boot slammed into his face, pressing his jaw into the ground. The man was definitely as big as a buffalo. And from his superior position, he could twist Matthias into an angle that disarmed all his power.

"I said don't move." Lefton kept his boot squarely positioned on Matthias's face as he made quick work of tying his hands. He muttered under his breath the whole time, but nothing coherent.

"There."

Finally, the boot lifted, and Matthias eased out the breath he'd been holding. His jaw ached now, too, but nothing compared to his leg.

The man grabbed his bound wrists and pulled upward, dragging Matthias back and sending that scalding poker iron through the joints where his arms met his shoulders. If he ever got loose from these ropes, he'd be tempted to kill the man.

Lefton pulled him backward, and Matthias staggered to his feet. He couldn't help a glance at Opal, who looked as though she might jump up and bolt forward to help him. Her arms were still tied behind her back, but he'd cut off the last of rope that tied her to the tree.

Run away. Now. He tried to tell her with his eyes, but the way Lefton half-dragged him, he couldn't be sure she saw anything besides his panic and pain. 'Twas time to make a strategy, or they'd both suffer a miserable death.

He had no doubt about Lefton's intentions now.

Opal had to make a plan.

Lefton finished tying Matthias to a tree at the edge of the clearing, then picked up the rifle and knife he'd thrown that direction. With both in hand, the man straightened and turned his focus to her, that crooked grin on his face.

Why was he doing this? The brute must be deranged. But he seemed to know exactly what he planned to do with them both, as though he'd plotted and schemed for months.

He kept his hungry gaze on her the entire time as he veered to the north end of the clearing where he'd first appeared from the woods, deposited Matthias's gun and knife on the ground, then picked up his own rifle and headed toward her.

'Twas hard not to cower against the tree as he advanced, his bulky form almost large enough to block out the sunlight as he towered above her.

"Now, let's see what's next for you, little lady." He lowered himself beside her, the stench of his presence filling her senses and churning bile in her midsection. "First off, we need to fix these ropes again."

He took up the cord and fiddled with it for several moments. Maybe if she could get him talking about whatever had happened five years ago, she might find a clue for how they could get away from him.

"Mr. Lefton, you mentioned something terrible that happened on the prairie five years ago. Did you lose someone special? Maybe your wife?" She held her breath as she watched for his face to mottle red again, the way it seemed to do when he was angry. This line of questioning could work, or, if she raised too many bad memories, it could make things infinitely worse.

He seemed to ignore her, as he focused on the rope. He was tying knots in it, probably refastening the pieces Matthias cut through.

She slid a glance at him across the clearing. Her chest ached at the pain he must be in. Forsooth, he'd been shot. 'Twas a wonder he could sit upright. He wasn't looking at her, but seemed to be staring at the ground around him. Perhaps, that was his way of dealing with his pain.

251

Forcing her gaze back to Lefton, she tried to study his face without making it obvious. Would he answer or did she need to find another way to coax him into talking?

But as she tried to formulate another question, he spoke, his voice low and bitter. "He killed my wife."

The words were so unexpected, 'twas a second before they sank fully into her thoughts. Matthias? He was such a good man, it was hard to imagine him killing anyone, especially a woman. But she'd best be careful how she questioned this madman.

Thankfully, he spoke again without her prompting. "We were on our way west, traveling with four other wagons. Thought there would be safety in numbers." That last comment seemed to drip with bitter regret, but he kept on.

"Night had just settled in and we was about to eat. I took the horses to water at the creek while Abigail finished cookin'. A patch of trees kept the whole thing hidden from me until I heard her scream. I came runnin'. Saw a swarm of half-naked redskins slippin' around like bees in a honey hive. One of 'em saw me comin' and sent a lead ball into my leg. Knocked me down, an' I hit my head on a rock."

He fingered the fresh-cut end of a rope. "Next thing I knew, I was wakin' up to more screams. All the Indians were still runnin' around, carryin' torches and settin' fire to things. I saw him then, your sweetheart." He shot her a look, his eyes so full of hatred, she had to clamp her jaw to keep from pulling back.

"He had my wife. Had her trussed up tight, and he was wavin' a fiery stick in her face. First, he lit her hair on fire, then he started her skirts flamin'." The man's voice graveled as the pain leached through it. "I tried to get to her. Tried to stop him. But my leg was busted up pretty bad, and I had to crawl. I threw rocks at him. Screamed at him. Screamed for the Almighty to save her. Then I watched the flames eat up her skin and burn her lifeless body."

A hardness had slipped over his voice. No doubt that was the only way he could bring himself to speak the memory, by turning the pain into anger. But this anger had consumed him, turning him into an ogre that would likely have horrified his poor wife.

Lefton seemed to pull himself from the memories with a jerk as he reached to secure the rope around her again.

But there was one more thing she had to get clear in her mind. "Mr. Lefton. I'm so sorry for all you and your Abigail suffered. No one should meet that kind of death, nor be forced to watch one they love endure it. But how do you know it was Matthias there with the Indians?"

He harrumphed as he jerked the rope tight around her middle, pinning her arms to her side again. "He was dressed up like a savage, but that blond hair stood out like a flag. The moment I saw him come in my livery a few years back, I knew 'twas him again."

"So his hair was what made you recognize him?" She tried to keep the incredulity out of her voice.

"That and the look of him. After watchin' him kill my wife, I'd know the lucifer anywhere."

She'd pressed far enough, so she pinched her mouth shut. But honestly, he was about to kill them both on the fact that Matthias shared the same hair color with a murderer? That and a vague recognition that could very possibly be wrong, given how distraught he must have been when the horrible massacre happened. Not to mention the pain from his leg and the befuddlement he must have experienced from hitting his head so hard.

And now, she and Matthias were to die because of this man's misguided anger. Maybe he just needed someone to blame. She could understand that. But it didn't mean she wanted to become his scapegoat.

He jerked the final knot tight and raised to his feet. "Stay put." He turned and retreated to the edge of the trees where he rummaged through a pack.

She took the opportunity to look at Matthias. He still sat by that tree, watching her with a look in his eyes that clogged a lump of emotion in her throat. His gaze bespoke encouragement. Love. Commitment.

Such a good man. Even with his own pain, he was reaching out to strengthen her with the only means allowed him—his gaze.

Lefton returned, carrying a stick about the length of his forearm, it's end wrapped in a cloth. His face wore a look of firm resolve as he knelt beside her again, then he took a small box out of his pocket.

He opened it and pulled out a match. Panic rose up in her throat, but she breathed hard to keep it at bay.

Holding the tiny piece up between them, she saw the first spark of remorse cross his face. "I warned you, Miss Opal, and now you see he's nothin' but an Indian-lovin' murderer."

If she'd had her hands free, she would have shaken the man. One last chance to work some sense into him before he became the murderer he accused Matthias of being.

He worked the match against the striker, and Opal took in long, slow breaths to keep herself from focusing on his intent. If she let herself imagine what it would feel like to burn to death, she'd lose any ability to think through a plan of escape.

She wanted to look to Matthias again, draw more strength from him, but she didn't want him to see the fear her own eyes surely reflected.

So as the tiny match flamed to life, then lit the cloth binding the torch…she prayed.

Matthias worked at the rope binding him to the tree, sawing at its thickness with his tiny boot knife. He had to twist his arms at such a harsh angle, it was hard to get the leverage he needed. But Opal's life depended on him getting loose, so he bent further and pushed the knife blade harder into the rope.

'Twas a miracle this knife had landed in a patch of grass where it was hidden from Lefton's view. Only something God could have orchestrated.

A spark of flame captured his attention where Lefton knelt beside Opal. His blood ran cold as the man held a long match against the cloth of his torch. His story had been a tragic one, but it didn't give him the right to torture and kill another human being. Especially not Opal.

He sawed harder at the rope, and could feel the threads of the cord breaking with each swipe. *God, please let me be in time. Help her. If you don't use me, save Opal a different way.*

The torch in Lefton's hand flared to life, flaming as though it had been dipped in kerosene. He moved it close to Opal's face

Matthias sawed harder, ignoring the cramps in his arms and wrist. Ignoring the burn in his leg. None of it would matter until he had Opal free of that revenge-hungry blackguard.

Even across the distance, he heard her gasp, drawing his focus again. Flames licked at the long golden braid hanging over her shoulder. His stomach balled in an acrid knot, and bile rose up his throat as he doubled his efforts at the rope. *God, help her.*

A whimper drifted to him, but he didn't let himself look. The moment he cut through this last rope, he would dive toward his rifle and knife where Lefton had placed them about a dozen feet away.

Opal screamed, igniting a frenzy inside him.

The rope broke under his knife blade, and he surged to his feet. His wounded leg tried to crumble, but he was prepared for that and kept his weight mostly on his good leg.

Lefton bellowed as Matthias leapt toward his weapons. He fit his hands in the familiar position on the rifle and spun on his knees to face the fiend.

But Lefton had already raised his own gun and sighted down the trigger.

In that instant, everything seemed to slow. He saw with a sudden clarity that he was about to die. *Into Your hands, Lord. But please don't let Opal suffer.*

A gunshot blasted.

Opal screamed.

Matthias pressed his eyes shut as the acrid smell of powder filled his mouth and nose. He waited for the force of the bullet to slam into him.

Chapter Twenty-Four

nother scream pierced the air. This one different from Opal's. Deeper.

Matthias opened his eyes to see Lefton rolling on his side on the ground, clutching his hand to his chest. His rifle lay on the ground near him, the barrel twisted awkwardly.

Matthias sprinted forward, keeping his own gun in a firing position. Aiming at the man writhing on the ground.

But he had to put out the fire that seemed to be spreading across Opal's shoulder, as though her coat had ignited. He veered around Lefton, keeping himself between the man and Opal.

When he reached her, he scanned her body to get a handle on the situation. The flames had licked halfway up her hair and across the shoulder of her coat. He had nothing to smother it with, save his own coat. Or maybe her skirt.

He used the one that would take the least amount of time, gathering the edge of her dress that flared around her and pressing it hard against the fire.

She screamed again, probably from the pain of his pressure against her burns. But he had to put out the flame.

He moved the cloth along her coat, extinguishing the fire everywhere he worked. At last, nothing remained except a trail of smoke and the stench of burned hair.

"Are you all right?" The sight of the charred remnants made bile churn in his gut, especially when he thought of the pain Opal must still be feeling. But he couldn't linger on it now.

"Fine. Take care of him." She motioned toward the man still lying on the ground.

He refocused the gun on Lefton, mere feet away from them.

The viper still clutched his soot-blackened hand, but he eyed Matthias with a wary gaze, enough hatred flashing in his eyes to keep Matthias on alert.

"You even twitch and I'll shoot you without a second thought." He waited for the words to sink in. "And for the record, I'm not the man who killed your wife. I'm sorry you both went through that, but I had nothing to do with it."

He didn't wait to see whether any of the hatred leeched from the man's gaze, just limped around him to retrieve his knife from the edge of the clearing. He had to get Opal untied, and he'd need the rope to secure their captive.

When he bent to pick-up the knife, a rustle in the woods made him straighten and aim the rifle that direction before he had time to think through his reaction. The shadows shifted into the form of a yellow-haired dog who limped from the trees into the clearing. Charmer?

"Look who it is." The dog walked right past Matthias, aiming for Opal. Smart animal. Matthias chuckled as he gathered his weapons and moved back to join the reunion.

Within minutes, he'd sliced through Opal's bindings, then had Lefton's hands and feet tied. He wasn't taking any chances that would allow the man to work himself loose. He extracted three knives from him and ignored the burns on his hands where the rifle's backfire had scorched him. They could deal with that in a few minutes.

Finally, at long last, he turned his attention to what really mattered.

Matthias straightened and looked to Opal, who knelt with the dog, still stroking it as the animal looked to be reveling in the attention. She met his gaze, fear and pain still lingering in her luminous blue eyes. Yet there was more. Relief. Concern. And as he stared into them, everything in her expression changed to love. She rose to her feet and stepped forward, then almost flew into his arms.

He took her in, wrapping her as tight as he dared, but careful not to touch the burned area.

"Matthias." She nestled in deeper, pressing her head into the crook of his neck.

The smell of fire rose up from her, reminding him again of how close he'd come to losing her. Tucking his face in her hair, he tried to force down the emotion clogging his throat.

"Did you hear what I said earlier? About why I came?"

His heart picked up speed again. He'd love to see her face, but he wasn't about to let her go. Still, maybe it would be better for her if she did. He leaned away to look in her eyes. "Maybe you'd be safer if you stayed in Mountain Bluff." He nodded toward the man tied on the ground. "After all, when people get too close to me, bad things tend to happen to them."

She took his face in both her hands, and he couldn't help but meet her fierce look. "That's a lie, and you know it. My safety is in God's hands, and I fully believe He brought me to you. Which means He's taking care of the details." The touch of a grin tweaked the corner of her mouth. "Including him." She nodded toward the same man, but kept her gaze on Matthias.

That thought seemed almost too good to believe. Had he been selling God short all this time? To think that a flawed man like him could have any real control over the good or bad that happened to others within God's plan. Considering it from this angle gave him an entirely different picture.

He pulled her close again, letting the idea settle over him. "Are you sure you think you can put up with me?

She chuckled, and he could feel the wonderful sensation through every part of him. "I think I'm up for the challenge."

He ran a hand up to stroke her head. At least the fire hadn't made it all the way up her braid. "I need to get you back to Mountain Bluff."

She pulled back to look at him, and he drank in those beautiful eyes. The way each delicate feature formed the perfect face of a woodland nymph. "Your knee. How are you even standing here? You were shot."

Funny how he'd forgotten about that pain while he held her in his arms. He ran a finger across her cheek. "Should we tend your burns now or wait and let the doc look at them?"

Her mouth curved in a gentle smile. "I'm fine. But you need a doctor. And so does he." She looked to Lefton, who lay on the ground, glaring at them.

He couldn't help himself any longer. She was too kind and beautiful and strong not to be kissed. As he lowered his mouth, she raised her face to meet him.

This kiss was the sweetest one yet.

They were a weary group when they straggled into Mountain Bluff that night. Matthias rode around to the front door of the boardinghouse and reined in their caravan, but he was loathe to dismount just yet.

Because Opal had been up all night, he'd suggested partway through the day that she tie her horse behind Lefton's mount and ride double with Matthias. He was pretty sure she'd been sleeping ever since, resting solidly against his back. The regular sound of her breathing had kept his heart in a steady beat of longing.

Soon, he'd get to spend every night listening to her breathe as she slept. He might never sleep again.

Although just now, with his leg aching something fierce, he could probably nod off for a week. But the first step was to dismount.

He turned to look back at the sullen man tied on his mount. "You sit tight. I'll send some folks back for you."

Lefton just glared.

Gathering his will power, he reached for Opal's hands locked around his waist and slowly unpeeled them.

She roused, sitting up with a sleepy yawn that almost made him sweep her into another kiss. "Are we here already?"

He couldn't help a chuckle. "We're here. Think you can get down, or should I carry you in?" Although if she opted for the latter, he'd be hard-pressed to oblige. He'd be doing good if his leg supported his own weight across the threshold, much less being responsible for someone who mattered so much more.

"I can walk." She slid off the side, and even in the darkness, he didn't miss her wince as she lowered herself. Her burns had to be worse than she'd let on.

As he dismounted, he kept a firm grip on the saddle until he could be sure he wouldn't collapse on the dirt. Opal's gentle hand slipped around his waist, and she fit herself under his arm. The support he needed, just like she was made for that place.

And he was pretty sure God had done just that.

A week later, Opal stood at the work counter in the kitchen, rolling dough so she could cut strips for sweet rolls. A place she'd stood hundreds of other mornings, yet nothing about today felt normal in the least.

This afternoon, she would become Mrs. Matthias Björk.

The kitchen door opened, and that very man stepped in, his face a little sheepish. Mrs. S.'s voice rang out from behind him. Something about a *guten morgen*.

When he saw her, he seemed to regain his composure, and that cocksure grin tipped his mouth as he strode toward her. She did her best to ignore him, although 'twas impossible not to feel the flurry in her midsection.

Especially when he stepped behind her and slipped his arms around her waist, then rested his chin on her shoulder. "Guten morgen." His deep, sleep-roughened voice sent a shiver down her arms.

She rested her hands on his at her waist. "Did Mrs. S. send you in here?"

He nuzzled her neck, his clean-shaven face smooth against her tender skin. "She might have talked me into it."

She sank into him, settling into his strength as he enveloped her. But then he straightened, forcing her to do the same. He moved around to face her, leaning against the edge of the work table. Something about the way he looked at her, all hint of happiness gone from his gaze, made all the flips in her middle come to a skidding halt.

She pressed her hand to his chest. "What is it? Does your leg pain you?"

He shook his head. Of course, she knew it still did, but his limp had been much better these last few days. He was still staring at her, though. Studying her.

Finally, he asked, "Are you sure about this?"

A pang of worry pressed her chest. "About what?" *Lord, don't let him have second thoughts. Please.*

Grooves had found their way across his forehead as he watched her. "About going north with me. Are you sure you want to leave all this? If it weren't so far, I'd go first and make sure everything's ready before I send for you."

She pressed both hands on his chest now and looked squarely into his eyes. "Of course, I'm sure. If you think I'd let you leave me behind, you've taken leave of your senses, Mr. Björk."

He searched her face, and she knew she needed to say more. "I'm sorry I was so fearful before. I couldn't see clearly what God had planned for me. For us."

His brows quirked up. "And now you see it? Please, do tell."

She couldn't help but smile at his sassiness. "I don't actually know the details. But I know what He's brought me through thus far, and He gave me this wonderful time with the Shumeisters. And then I met you." She gave his chest a little poke. "When I see how He's brought good out of my bad already, how can I not trust that He'll bring me to something even better. "'For I know the thoughts that I think toward you,' saith the Lord, 'thoughts of peace, and not of evil, to give you an expected end.'"

His eyes searched her face again. "I don't want you to regret your choice."

She met his gaze. "I've already experienced the regret of staying behind and I'm not willing to go through that again. I have no doubt going with you will bring its share of emotions, but regret won't be among them." Then she reached up on her tiptoes and kissed him. Just so he would know she meant every word.

His response was quick and sure, deepening the kiss with an intensity that took her breath away, leaving her spinning in a world where nothing existed besides him.

At last, he pulled back the slightest bit, resting his forehead on hers as their breathing mingled. She touched his cheek, rubbing her thumb across his chin and jaw. "And you can be sure, sir, that our expected end should contain a great deal more of that."

His mouth tipped in that roguish grin. "A great deal more."

Epilogue

SEPTEMBER, 1868 ~ EIGHT MONTHS LATER
HOT SPRINGS CAMP, CANADIAN ROCKIES

*D*earest Tori,

So much has happened since I last wrote, I pray you'll pardon my rambling as I catch you up on the details. They say winter is coming here in the mountain country, but I confess, I'm not sure we ever truly experienced summer.

Alanna seems much recovered already since we arrived two months ago. She dotes on Matthias, and he teases her endlessly, so that I'm surprised she doesn't send him away at times. Yet, the affection between them is so strong, it makes me miss you all the more, dear cousin.

But I don't begrudge Matthias these treasured moments with his sister, as he missed so much time in their youth. It makes me thankful, Tori, for every day we spent together at Riverdale, although I've not been accustomed to thankfulness for that time. Yet no matter what we experienced, we had each other for comfort and cheer. I thank our Heavenly Father daily for you.

And how is my little namesake? Do you remind her often of her auntie? Please give her a hug and tell her only the good stories of me. The thought of this missed time with her brings tears to my eyes.

But, I confess, almost everything brings on tears these days. Like when I found a nest of snowshoe hares last week. The little rabbits were so tiny and curious, with their noses twitching at me. I cried all the way home, every time I pictured their innocent faces.

Alanna has great patience with my weeping and has experienced it more than once as we sit in the hot springs each day. For her, the foul-smelling mineral in the water seems to be curing her ailment. For me, I simply relish the time resting my swollen limbs.

Did I tell you in my last letter the baby has begun to move inside me? Nay, more than move. This young Björk lad has already taken up his father's antics. Matthias seems humored by it, but he'll get his full taste when the child is born. I only pray the babe is safe, and that he doesn't come out bearing Matthias's broad shoulders. Not at first, that is. He can grow into them.

In truth, Tori, this life God blessed us with is full of excitement, yet I've learned that I'm also safe. Tucked within my Father's hands and nestled next to Matthias, there is nothing that can shake me. Nothing that can alter our Lord's plans.

Love to you and all our family,
Opal

Did you enjoy this book? I hope so!

Would you take a quick minute to leave a review?
http://www.amazon.com/dp/B073W3NTFY

It doesn't have to be long. Just a sentence or two
telling what you liked about the story!

~ ~ ~

Receive a FREE short story and get updates when
new Misty M. Beller books release:
http://eepurl.com/bXmHwb

About the Author

 **Misty M. Beller** writes romantic mountain stories, set on the 1800s frontier and woven with the truth of God's love.

She was raised on a farm in South Carolina, so her Southern roots run deep. Growing up, her family was close, and they continue to keep that priority today. Her husband and daughters now add another dimension to her life, keeping her both grounded and crazy.

God has placed a desire in Misty's heart to combine her love for Christian fiction and the simpler ranch life, writing historical novels that display God's abundant love through the twists and turns in the lives of her characters.

Sign up for e-mail updates when future books are available!
www.MistyMBeller.com

Don't miss the other books in
Misty M. Beller's
Wyoming Mountain Tales

Book 1

Amazon.com/dp/B01LXP8PNL

Book 2

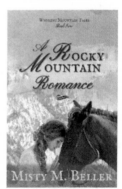

Amazon.com/dp/B01MQYOL58

Book 3

Amazon.com/dp/B06XNN8XQV

Also look for

Misty M. Beller's

Mountain Dreams Series:

Book 1

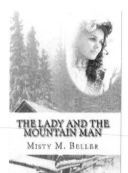

Amazon.com/dp/B00MQB7F4U

Book 2

Amazon.com/dp/B00T8XN9Q2

Book 3

Amazon.com/dp/B00WH8RBPA

Book 4

Amazon.com/dp/B011GC7VHA

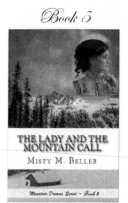

Also look for:
Misty M. Beller's
Texas Rancher Trilogy:

Book 1

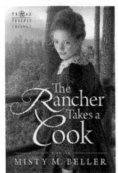

Amazon.com/dp/B01064BQCU

Book 2

Amazon.com/dp/B010EN1YSO

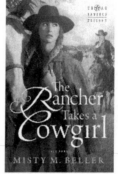

And the new series:

Misty M. Beller's

Heart of the Mountains:

Book 1

Amazon.com/dp/B074J72XDH

78982318R00171

Made in the USA
Columbia, SC
23 October 2017